HIDDEN ABOVE HER

PART ONE

KANDLE BOSSFIELD

PUBLISHED BY POYS PUBLISHING

Published by POYS Publishing, an imprint of The Khaidence House (USA), 2016

ISBN: 978-0-578-50094-2

DEDICATION

To my sons, Joshua and Khaidence.
Always give it your best shot, even
when you clean your room.

— Mom

ACKNOWLEDGMENTS

I would like to say thank you to my beta team and early readers for all your support. I also want to give a special thank you and shout-out to my editors: Good Reid's Editing Service, Maddy D., Lyssa Dawn Author Services, and Horus Proofreading. I am certainly grateful for all your help with editing and proofreading.

THE TRUTH

I *s he trying to kill me?*
    I plop down on the chair and throw my fore-
head into the palms of my hands. *Don't cry.* I
squeeze my eyes and envision packing my bags
with a smile, because in twenty-four hours, I'll be
on a plane to Los Angeles. But there's a problem.

I open my eyes and turn around. The dirty
body is on the kitchen floor with messy, blonde
hair and blood dripping from her nose. Any intelli-
gent person would leave right now, but I can't. Not
until I get what I deserve. Not until I get the truth.

The marijuana smoke drifts from the bud on
the floor, and it's drying the saliva on my tongue.
I cough, and my black heels clunk on the bamboo
floor as I walk over to the French balcony and slide
open the door. The cars hum below as they maneuver through the morning traffic on J Street. I step
out and place my hands on the cold and bumpy
metal rail.

Why hasn't he called?

The icy wind cools down my almond skin and
blows through my thick, kinky hair, which tickles

my elbows. The sun's a highlight of orange on the verge of a little February rain. I look across the street at the concrete building. It has a restaurant below called the Mexican Grill, written in big, bold, blue letters. State workers move fast on both sides of the downtown Sacramento streets, which consists of women in business dresses with tennis shoes on and men with business attire and suitcases. City buses roll by, and the parking enforcement is busy setting up the area with cones for construction work.

Speaking of work, I remember how it took me six stupid months to find my wedding dress. Thinking back, I remember how my heart thumped, and how my palms shook in nervousness. I was engaged for the very first time, happy of course, but from time to time, doubt still tapped me on the shoulders. I stood up on the panel in front of the large mirror, and I was speechless when I admired the beautiful, ivory ball gown draped in crystals and lace, which lifted my boobs in all the right places. But most of all, my mother cried. It takes a lot for my mother to show emotion. She's always so nonchalant, and you can never guess what she's thinking. So to witness that sour-faced, snot cry for the first time, I knew it touched her heart. So how am I going to explain to her what's happening right now?

It's crazy how a few seconds could change someone's life. It only takes a few seconds to get hit by a bus, a few seconds to lose everything in a poker game, and a few seconds to break an ankle running in a track meet.

It's been ten minutes since I opened my fiancé's apartment door and saw the blonde girl cooking eggs in blue lingerie. *Life- changing? Definitely, and it only took a few seconds to realize that I had to call off my freaking wedding!*

Confusion shoves hard at my chest. *Come on. Get it together.* I put the tip of my thumb underneath my fingers to activate the spinner in the middle. The mini-chain races inside the titanium ring. The vibration is soothing, which causes the constant gasp in my breath to stop. My mother thought I had a rare breathing disorder that caused me to breathe this way. My dad called it asthma, but in reality, it's good old-fashioned anxiety that creeps up from time to time. Yup, this is my life. This ring makes me feel in control, even though everything in front of me is out of my control.

I turn and peek back inside at the blonde girl on the floor. She looks nothing like me. She has a pointy nose, long chin, and a fake basketball butt attached to her baseball-bat legs. Oh, and I can't forget the artificial cantaloupes on her chest. I have high cheekbones, full lips, a flat stomach, and my once-meaty thighs are now thinned out and toned. My breasts resemble succulent oranges, but they aren't as perky as other twenty-two-year-olds my age. But they're absolutely perfect for Sym. Yup, that's me... Symphony "Sym" Dunmore. But I prefer Sym to differentiate between the old, youthful Symphony and the grown ass adult Sym that I am now. Yup, I'm an adult, but I never thought I would have a day like today.

This morning, I woke up to a call from a frantic girl who said my fiancé, Todd, was going to die, and then she hung up. At first, I thought, 'Why would a little girl be calling me?' Todd doesn't have any little sisters. She had to have been at least a teenager, because she had such a small voice. I immediately called Todd, and of course, he didn't answer. So I called his boss and found out he no longer worked for the law firm, which was odd because he didn't mention it to me when we took engagement photos at the park the other day. So I woke up my sister-cousin, Tevah, to come with me to his condo. Tevah's my ride or die. You know, the closest person to me who is ready to pray, fight, or twerk with me at the drop of a dime.

I stuck my emergency key into the apartment door and expected to find him in a pool of blood, but nope —no him, and no blood. Instead, Tevah and I stepped into a game of Who Doesn't Belong. And the forty-million-dollar question was: was it the blonde girl sucking on a blunt and cooking in the kitchen, or me?

I asked the blonde what the hell she was doing in my man's condo. She disregarded my question and told me Todd took off in her daddy's new Porsche, and her father would kill Todd if he saw him driving it. Yeah, I know what you're thinking, this is some twisted shit, but it gets better. Never mind the fact that she played a part in destroying my relationship and forget about the twenty-by-twenty-four-inch photo hanging by the front door of us gazing into each other's eyes. All she wanted was my help to get her daddy's car back?

I got in her face, called her fifty-two sluts, and told her she left her brain back at the whorehouse she came from. Her stinky dragon breath almost made me pass out. I couldn't believe the audacity of this girl to feel comfortable enough to cook here and ask me, of all people, for help. I've never been in this type of confrontation before. But for my first skirmish encounter, I thought I did rather well, until the blonde yelled back. She said something along the lines of how I should be thankful she kept my fiancé satisfied and asked, sarcastically, if I liked the lingerie my fiancé bought her with my credit card. That moment turned into unbelievable silence because those words knocked my soul right out of my skin.

It's been nine minutes since Tevah punched the blonde in the face, using all the power from her tattooed submachine arm. She hit her so hard that the blonde tripped over my foot and smashed her face on the tan rock floor in the kitchen. She has yet to move and could possibly be dying. But I'm too distraught about my relationship to care about her problems. I hate confrontation; anytime I can avoid it, I will, but I have someone with me who is always ready to punch confrontation in the throat, and her name is Tevah.

"Sym, snap out of it," Tevah says with a frown on her round face. Her thick gold chain dangles around her neck as she struts in her Jordan sneakers. I love my sister-cousin. Tevah has vanilla-cookie skin, hairy arms, and her ocean-blue eyes are like stretched ovals like her mother, whom we only saw in pictures. Her blue hair is very short in the back and her choppy bangs are long. I'm sure by tomorrow her hair will either be purple or red. She has thin-arched eyebrows and thick, robust legs that never jiggle in her size-six-teen, cut-off jean shorts. She wears a pink fanny pack around her waist. And her *"you must be crazy if you don't think I'm sexy walk"* makes all the boys stare. Tevah marches back into Todd's room, now with scissors in hand.

Oh, gosh.

Tevah and I are cousins but were raised like sisters. We look nothing alike, but we favor our mothers. Tevah's mom is of European descent, and my mother is of African-American descent. And our fathers are both of Samoan descent.

When we were kids, Tevah climbed trees and pushed around the neighborhood boys while I sat on the porch, setting up a full-on wedding production for afro-Barbie, so she could marry her man, Kendrick. After the blonde made those accusations about my credit card, Tevah's top lip curled, and there was nothing I could do. I've seen that look before.

I wish I were more like her—so fearless of consequences. I'm the youngest out of Tevah and my brother, Duck, and they always act as if their job is to protect me, even though I'm more than capable of defending myself.

I tend to keep things all sealed up in a jar sometimes. Tevah reminds me at least once a month, of how life's too short not to act on how I feel. She lost her parents in a tragic car accident, so her views on life are more cutthroat than mine. Finding out about what happened to her parents turned her into a no-nonsense kind of girl. Her perception of the world is black and white. There's no gray area. The answer's either a yes or no in her world. Last year, after graduating, Tevah moved in with a roommate in Los Angeles. But now, her roommate's boyfriend is moving in, so Tevah and I are getting a place together. We already put down a deposit for our apartment out there, so she's in town to help me move. We don't have furniture yet, but we'll make a quick stop at the Furniture-4-U store, and we'll be good to go. Moving together was supposed to be temporary until after Todd and I got married next year. I guess those plans got thrown out the window this morning.

I leave the patio door open and walk back into the living room. My skinny jeans brush against the corner of the GQ Magazine on the coffee table. Something flies, cracks, and slides across the wooden floor. It's a CD with a shadowy silhouette of a curvy woman with wavy hair standing in front of a blue background. I bend down, and my hair brushes over my chest. I have been searching for this CD for weeks now. It's of the artist H.E.R, which means, *Having Everything Revealed.* She's an R&B songstress who keeps her persona a mystery, rocking sunglasses and long, curly hair to conceal

13

most of her face on a dark stage. I know it's my CD because she wrote me a note on the back. It says, *Symphony, Follow your dreams. Sincerely, H.E.R.* I remember playing her CD in my car when I picked Todd up from the airport a few weeks ago. He never asked to borrow it, but it somehow ended up between the pages of a magazine in his apartment? Maybe he has plans to give it back.

I'm talking about a successful lawyer who showers me with stilettos, purses, clothes—you name it. The cost never mattered to him. But facts are, he has a woman in his apartment, and my Visa card has been missing since I left it on my dresser at home, in my room. Facts are, Todd was the last person around me when I had it, and he insisted I hold off on reporting it lost. Now that I think about it, he was so confident it would show up. *Could that have been a distraction?* Now I'm second-guessing myself. Of course, Todd has money, he paid for my ivory wedding gown. He paid six thousand dollars to be exact. Yup, six thousand dollars for a dress that I'm going to wear once, but it's a shame that I still pretended to be happy with the most manipulative, egotistical, "hog the bathroom to look pretty" man I ever met. Sort of like how I'm pretending there's a possibility the blonde might be alive in the kitchen.

I walk into Todd's bedroom. I jolt back. The explosion of movement in Todd's closet startles me. I don't know what Tevah's doing in there. But I'm sure it's something to make me feel better. *Is this happening right now?* I sit at the foot of the bed. My rapid heartbeat disrupts my unsettling emotions with a mixture of disgust and confusion, which impales my bones. I hope Tevah's in there swinging like a professional golfer. Speaking of a career.

Getting hired as a celebrity news correspondent has always been my dream. I interviewed by phone three times at the Hollyview Network in Los Angeles. If hired, I'll be eligible to join the prestigious creative board, which is a team that selects the actresses and models for the featured sitcoms on the network.

My mission is to eliminate the body-shaming perception that women need to be thin to fit into the entertainment world. The standard of beauty is drastically different. There are so many women who run to get plastic surgery to appear like the ideal woman the network portrays to be perfect. You know, the girl who eats a piece of lettuce for breakfast, a grape for lunch, and a slice of a raisin for dinner. I want young girls to know beauty comes in all shapes and sizes. I feel if I don't do something about it now, young girls growing up may think it's not cool to be comfortable in their own skin. I've been there before. It's a dark place to be when you can't stand gazing at all the bumpy grooves of your body in the mirror, all because some peanut-headed loser at school doesn't like your body and tells everyone how he feels.

I want to show women, whether they're tall,

short, plump, or wide, that it's all about the confidence that makes a woman sexy. It's about how secure a woman feels about herself, because when a woman gets to a certain level of security, she will not need a man to validate her sexiness. *You know what I mean?* But there's one problem. The thought of being on television, in front of the world, tightens the thick rope of anxiety around my neck. But I'm ready to hop out the plain, white box I've been walking in circles in all these years.

I look around. I'm not exactly certain of what I'm looking for, but my intuition tells me to continue. Sadly enough, I can't pretend like everything's fine, even though I want to, but I can't this time.

My mother always says, *When people get engaged, most secrets come out.* There's something about the stress of planning a wedding that brings out the worst part of a person, sometimes skeletons pop out of the closet too. Some people choose to ignore it, and others take a run for it. It's like God exposes every flaw the other person has in the open, like a test... the "can you live with this person for the rest of your life" kind of test. If this is my test, I'm failing and will gladly write a big, fat ass X over our future together, unless maybe, I want to keep pretending. *But why would I do that? Maybe I just want to prove to my parents that I'm mature enough to control my own life?* I sigh.

The shiny, black drawer grabs my attention. I push off the bed and carefully rummage through boxer briefs. A SMUD bill and an open letter from the Internal Revenue Service? *Two hundred fifty thousand dollars owed?* I swallow. *This can't be right. Why didn't he tell me about this?* It's from a year ago, so maybe he's cleared up the misunderstanding by now. I look down. *Credit cards?* I pick up the Visa card with the name Ryan Bracey, the MasterCard, Allen Desmond, and the Discovery card, Victor Peterson? *Why do all these names sound familiar?* I throw them on the bed. He has more than enough money. *Did he steal all these cards?*

The loud groaning from the kitchen drowns out my thoughts.

"Can you keep it down?" I yell out. I guess the blonde chicken in the kitchen isn't dead after all. But she certainly had a well-warranted beat-down.

"Tevah!"

"What's up?" she yells from the closet.

"Look at what I found," I calmly say and point to the credit cards lying on the bed.

Tevah walks out of the closet slightly winded. "What's this?"

"Look at the credit card names, do they sound familiar?"

She examines it. "Ryan Bracey, Allen Desmond, Victor Peterson," she says lazily. She points at one particular card. "The last four on this card are the same numbers I use to unlock my phone. Humph."

"Help!" The blonde girl weeps from the kitchen.

Tevah yells, "Shut up! Don't make me come over there! Todd's always bragging about what he's going to buy. I just knew he was into some illegal shit!" Tevah scrunches her eyebrows before leaving the room.

I pull the phone out of my back pocket and check my credit card account. My legs turn to feathers. There's a Victoria's Secret purchase from two days ago. The phone buzzes, and Todd's smiling photo pulls up on the screen. I want to reject the call, but avoiding this is like pretending a fifty-foot elephant isn't taking a massive dump on the bed. I back against the wall and press the green button.

SLEIGH RIDES

"*Hello?*" *I see a pale, tan hand and then gray covers the screen. I can hear the honking vehicles in the background. Did he accidentally call me?*

"Todd!" I yell.

Todd's face appears on the screen. He runs his hand over his short black hair, and through his serious expression, he forces a smile, showing his perfectly white teeth. Despite how mad I am at him, I can't help but notice how his muscles flex underneath his white dress shirt. He peers back at me with something to fear in his eyes, almost resembling a child caught with his hand in the cookie jar.

"Hold on, Sym. Don't say anything," he says anxiously, his bushy eyebrows up. I catch a glimpse of the Porsche emblem before the screen goes black.

"Hola," Todd says in Spanish and sniffs hard. "You got the sleigh ride?" Todd says in his deep voice.

"You know I got it. Hand it over," says a guy

with a squeaky voice. I press mute on the screen.

"Tevah, what's a sleigh ride?"

"Cocaine!" she yells from the living room.

"What did you say?"

"Drugs," she says. This is way too much for one day. Please let him be auditioning for a movie or something. Please.

The tires screech in the background. Todd's face appears on the screen. I press unmute.

"Todd, was that a freaking drug transaction?"

"Of course not. How's my Kitty?" he says, slurring his words.

"Todd, whose car are you driving?" I knew the answer to this, but I need to hear the truth come out of his mouth.

Crazy how there's a tiny part of me wishing everything was a stupid misunderstanding.

"It's a Porsche! My car's in the shop, so my mechanic loaned me a car for the weekend. I always wanted to drive one of these!" he says without a care in the world.

This story could sound believable if his black Mustang wasn't parked outside.

He lightly bites down on his bottom lip giving me that "I want to have sex" look. I tilt my head. The whites in his eyes are baby pink with red lightning stripes.

I say, "are you high on something?"

"Heck no!" He wipes the sweat from his forehead and squeezes his Rudolph-red nose. He's wearing a red, rubber strap on his wrist, and it has a red oversized bezel, the size of a closed fist. Did he buy another Magoose watch? It's a twenty-five-thousand-dollar watch. Why would he do that when we're saving for a house? I had to pay for dinner after his card was declined a few weeks ago. He paid me back, but his card was rejected again at the ice-cream shop.

He blows out a sigh in exhaustion. "I've been so busy preparing for my new case. Did you finish packing already?" He licks his lips. "I miss you."

The ruckus from the living room makes me jolt back to the current situation.

"What's that noise? Who's arguing?" Todd shouts desperately, trying to look into the background.

Tevah marches in the bedroom, holding a box of rat poison and a box of Lucky Charms cereal with irritation on her face. I snatch the rat poison out of her hand and shake my head. Tevah grabs the phone.

Tevah's expression causes Todd's eyes to slowly open like a garage door. "You were never good enough for my sister! And guess what... I'm going to hook her up with a guy with ten times the package! And you better give my sister back her credit card, you cheating motherfucker! That's why my dad doesn't like yo' ass!" she says in a rough-pitched tone and sprays saliva everywhere. She flares her diamond-studded nose and passes me back the phone. She pours the Lucky Charms all over the white bed, walks over to the nightstand, pushes the liquor bottles and shot glasses, and it splatters brown liquid artwork on the closet door.

His mouth gets wider than a rubber band. "I'm pulling over. Let me be clear. I'd shoot a fucking priest if he laid hands on you. I don't know what I'd do if I ever saw you with another man. I can't stomach such a thing. You know what I'm saying?" He clenches his jaw.

There's a better chance of watching a kangaroo Crip walk on the Ellen show before I ever marry this guy. I move my green shirt up and down to stop from overheating.

"I don't know what she's talking about. I'm not cheating on you! Tell me what's going on, Sym!"

"Are you sure you're not cheating on me?" I say sarcastically.

"Sym, is this about your fat-girl insecurities?" I gasp.

"My fat-girl insecurities? That's the only thing you can come up with to explain your actions— bringing up my past?" I say, walking toward the kitchen. I turn the camera view around. I want him to get a good view at his new blonde girl-friend with the swollen eye and dirty, red lipstick smudged all over her face and all on his kitchen floor like a murder scene.

"How about you justify why this drunk excuse of a woman is laying on your kitchen floor? In an outfit you bought her, with my credit card?"

Tevah slaps the blonde to wake her drunk

ass back up. "Yuck, she smells like she bathes in brown liquor," Tevah says with a sickened expression.

Todd says, "wait a minute... you're in my apartment?"

"Keep her away from me!" the blonde shouts and covers her face and bends her body in a fetal position. Tevah stands over her with her best annoyed Al Pacino expression.

"So do you want to tell me again how you did me a favor by having sex with my fiancé?" I say, raising an eyebrow.

"No, no!" The blonde quickly shakes her head.

"How'd you get a key?" Todd asks.

He has full-blown evidence of betrayal bleeding on his kitchen floor, and he's worried about how I got a key to his condo?

The blonde tries to struggle out of Tevah's grasp.

"Tevah, let go of her hair," I say.

If my eyes could chop, Todd's head would be rolling around on the passenger side in that fancy Porsche right about now. He uses his palm and nervously slides it from his hairline to the back of his neck. "Sym, I gotta be honest with you. She's a hurricane survivor. She needed a place to stay. I was going to tell you, but I knew you would act like this! Why don't you trust me?"

The girl groans. "Todd, give me back my daddy's car and my twenty grand, and I'll go. I promise."

"Twenty grand? For what?!" Tevah and I say simultaneously.

"Are you saying your daddy's your pimp?" Tevah asks.

The blonde nods. "What?" I shout.

Tevah and I throw both arms up like "you have got to be kidding me" shoe strings. "You paid twenty thousand dollars for sex?" I mutter in shock.

"You could go down to Stockton Boulevard for less than that," says Tevah.

I put my hand on my hip. "Tevah, stop."

Those words spread thick layers of mud all over my skin. I need an ob-gyn, eighty showers, and a bottle of blue mouthwash.

"Let me try to get this right. You slept with a prostitute, and you stole my credit card?" I stare at him like he had a hairy spider crawling out of his nose. He looks away.

"Oh, and I can't forget about the two hundred and fifty thousand dollars you owe the IRS, but you spent your money on prostitutes, and what, drugs? Are you freaking serious?" I stick out my neck.

"Hell no," he says, as if I was in violation of the law.

At this point, something must be wrong with me for agreeing to marry such an idiot.

"Sym, I never touched that girl!"

Planning his execution would make me smile right now. But I don't want to spend my life in some prison braiding some buff girl's hair.

"Todd, it's over between us."

"What?!" he shouts, as if I'm overreacting.

Tevah walks out of the living room in a hurry, like she's just remembering something.

Todd looks down. "Do you know how much money I spent on you? Do you think I'll let you leave me? Think about it... who would even want an ex-fat girl with stretch marks anyway? You're my charity work, you know what I'm sayin'?" he says with arrogance gleaming in his eyes.

"Stretch marks? Charity work?" *Those words sting the last piece of love in my heart.*

"Come on, Sym. I didn't mean that. Let's sit down and talk about this."

Tevah barges back into the living room, waving a piece of paper like she found the golden ticket, and in the other hand is a credit card. "Tell me it ain't so!" she says. "Diamond Cuts & Company. Sym, this is your engagement ring receipt! Purchased with the last four digits I use to unlock my phone!" She holds up the credit card. "Ryan Bracey bought your ring, not Lover Whore on the phone there."

"You bought my engagement ring with a stolen credit card?" I ask and tilt my head to the side.

The swinging ceiling light knocks my memory back.

"Isn't Ryan Bracey the cop you defended last year? The guy they put away for covering up that hotel murder? Let me try to get this right. Your client gets locked up, so you steal his credit card?"

He ogles me with hungry-puppy eyes. He sniffs and wipes his nose. "This is unacceptable! The diamond company must have given me someone else's receipt. I'm going to call them and clear all this up, I promise."

"You didn't answer the question, and I guess you're too coked out to realize you just lost the best woman you've ever had." I sigh.

"Sym, I got disbarred last year. Someone lied and said they found some drugs on top of my desk. So I'm under a lot of pressure, alright! I've been pretending to go to work because I thought I'd find a job before you caught on. I wanted to continue to provide you with the things you deserve. I did this for you. I did this for us," he pleads.

"No, you did it for *you*!" He sniffs hard like he stuffed a sleigh ride up his nose before he called. He quickly lifts his arm and uses the side of a black gun to scratch the side of his head. A gun? My stomach drops, but I act like I'm unfazed.

Tevah is pacing around laughing at how ridiculous this is. She didn't see the gun.

"Come on, Sym! Do you think I'll let you leave me just like that? What? You're going to go slut off with Cash now? I got something for Cash." He rubs his head with the gun again.

"Oh, please, my father has ten of those," I say. The same eyes that used to gleam with so much love were now empty and unfamiliar. I haven't seen my best friend Cash in years, yet Todd has always been jealous because we've kept in touch by phone.

Todd admires the gun. "Yeah, I got something for him." Todd has met my father, so I know he's not crazy enough to come to my house with that gun.

"Todd, it's over."

"Sym, I swear if I ever catch you with another man—"

"Todd, hold on. Somebody's calling on the other line, and guess what? He has ten times the package!" I press the red button to save my ears from whatever else he had to say with his contaminated tongue.

Tevah folds her arms. "Let's stick a needle in his office chair to deflate his balls! Sym, could you be pregnant by this clown?" I close my eyes and take a breath.

MOUNT FORTY

*I*t's been five *minutes since we left Todd's condo, and he's already called me ten times. I send the call to voicemail and block his number. Drops of water splash on the front window like a typewriter at twenty words a minute and Tevah is driving my black Kia like a madwoman. Why did I let her drive? Thank God for stoplights. We squeal to a stop at a red light.*

Todd and I have been intimate many times, and not once have I ever suspected he viewed my body as flawed.

When I was a baby, Mom said I had the cutest chubby cheeks. When I got to high school, I had meaty turkey legs like the kind you get from the county fair. But when I got older, my cheekbones were high and more defined when my fluffy face thinned out. Oh, and I can't forget how my stomach resembled a woman in her third trimester of pregnancy. I used to think, 'God, why me?' I would have rather had the slender body and a pudgy face, not viceversa—not because I was a big girl, but it was because I could never find any clothes that fit me just right. People would observe my body with an expression of concern, but when they got to my face, they'd say, "Oh, you're pretty." Like big girls were incapable of being beautiful.

I loved every bit of my voluptuousness, until the summer after I graduated high school. I decided to change out of my nightclothes to pick up a chocolate milkshake from Suzie's Burgers, and I struggled to zip up my stretchy jean pants for forty-five minutes. My stomach refused to move the freak over. Crazy thing is, the more I tried to lose weight, the more I gulped down chocolate milkshakes. I know, it sounds crazy. I spent most mornings affirming my beauty in the mirror, but I finally decided to make a change when going up and down those stairs at home became a huffing-and-puffing match. So I put on some old fitness tights and started walking around Mount Forty. I would power walk on my street and see Todd sitting on his mother's porch with his eyes glued to his cell phone, but I never spoke to him until one day he caught up to me and begged to join me. I never intended to work out as hard as I did, but Todd's encouragement helped me work harder.

It's weird how the same person who watched me overcome my biggest obstacles is the same person who just slammed my past in my face. After three years of dating, I introduced Todd to my family a few weeks ago. They were pissed off and saying we were rushing things. I tried to convince them that Todd was the perfect man to marry, but they acted like accepting him was like allowing a deer to join a pack of wolves.

After what happened today in Todd's apartment, I expect a machine gun of *"I told you so"* accusations to shoot my way.

"Shit!" Tevah shouts.

"I meant to pour magnesium in his sugar. Sym, stop trippin'. I'm going to roll up a big, fat ass blunt!"

That's one of the reasons I love her. Todd cheating on me is like Todd cheating on her. And it gives me comfort that I'm not going through this by myself.

"No, thanks. You know I don't smoke," I whisper.

"Tevah, stop!" I step on the imaginary brake pedal on my side and the blood rushes through my foot.

The tires skid to a complete halt. An old man steps off the curb, holding an old woman's hand a few seconds into our yellow light. They slowly stroll across the street with an umbrella. Oh my God! I really have to cancel my wedding.

My tough exterior tumbles. I am bare and exposed to every bit of my reality, and it's sitting in my chest. I inhale grief and exhale life without him. My hands tremble when I try to compose myself, but the ball of disbelief in my throat chokes me up.

My sobs resemble a three-year-old little girl who fell off a bike and busted her knee, only it's my heart that's busted. My tears overwhelm the napkin so much that my shirt saturates in two cups of warm, salty disappointment. But worst of all, I'm confused because I don't know if I'm more distraught over Todd cheating, the fact that I didn't know he did drugs, or my canceled wedding.

To be honest, my dream wedding exceeded the love I had for Todd, which is horrible because once the honeymoon was over, there wouldn't have been anything left to keep me thrilled.

But I can still hear my mother say, "Symphony, I don't want you out there sinning. Get married, give me some grandbabies, and do things the right way."

I'm more upset with myself that I had to go through this to realize he wasn't the one at all. It's like I purposely ignored the signs. And I wanted to walk down the aisle for what... to please my mom and dad? They wanted me married, but not to him.

"Sym, don't cry. I would kill to be a size six. You should be proud of yourself," Tevah says with her free hand rubbing my back.

"That's not it. Do you know how long I've dreamed of wearing a wedding dress? I never thought Todd would have done this to me. I didn't give up my virginity so he could throw me in a pile of old clothes on a chair. Thank God I always made him wear a condom. I never wanted to be the girl that got oopsy-poopsy pregnant by accident."

Tevah has a devilish smile and says, "Well, if it makes you feel better, unfortunately, you can't wear a wedding dress now, but Todd can't wear his expensive suits anymore!"

"Why?"

"I cut the arms off every single dress coat and shirt in his closet."

"That's what you were doing in there?"

I snicker and blow my nose hard into a tissue. She nods.

One thing Tevah can't stand is a cheating man. Her ex-boyfriend, Jon-Jon, is probably somewhere still recovering after she cut him last year for cheating on her. I bet she wishes she never gave up her virginity to him too.

I lost my virginity a lot later than my friends in high school because I'd been groomed to believe sex before marriage was a one-way ticket to hell. *"It's in the Bible," my mother used to tell me.*

The stories kept changing over the years though. She told me if I had sex before marriage, my vagina would fall out, and the government hadn't found a cure to help all the fallen vaginas of the world. But in the fifth grade, I found out it was a lie after I watched a sex education video in class. Somehow, those stories always stuck with me, which is probably why I've never experienced the hype of the significant "O" that everyone talks about. I always felt guilty after Todd and I had sex. As if I was doing something wrong.

"Orgasms are for married folks," my mother used to say. I twirl my engagement ring around my finger. "I'm tempted to throw this out the window."

"No, you're about to graduate! You have a student loan to pay. It's not going to pay itself. Give it to me. I'll sell it." I place the ring in her palm.

Great. She's going to sell a stolen ring, but I'm too weak to argue.

"Sym, it's not your fault he's a lying bastard! I should've peed on his bathroom plant. But believe me, you're going to find somebody better looking, and Todd will be crying alone in a corner somewhere," she says, turning the steering wheel.

"Right now, I want to lie under my blanket and eat Red Vines. I'll finish packing later," I say, sucking in the fresh-rain smell.

"Cash is going to flip when he hears about what happened. I bet Cash secretly still loves you, Sym. Maybe all this happened because you're supposed to be with him." She passes me an optimistic side-eye.

"Cash would be surprised about what happened today, but we're strictly friends. I'm like one of the guys. I know about the money-hungry groupie girls who stalk him when he's on tour. It took us a while to get where we are. Why ruin a good thing? Plus, I'm starting to think there's no such thing as fate. Why would fate want me to feel this way? Maybe I'm not meant to be with anybody. Maybe I'll be alone forever."

"Wow, that's depressing, but I'm pretty sure if I left you in a hotel room with Justin Timberlake or Thomas Q. Jones, you'd be back in love and pregnant before sunrise!"

"Well, that's different," I say with a grin. That's

what big sisters are for, right? Even on my worst days, she can force a smile out of me.

She has this mischievous look on her face. "Since we both don't have a man now, how about we do things the old-fashioned way!"

"Tevah, what are you talking about?"

"Remember when mom told us about asking God for signs?"

"Yeah, I remember. Isaiah 7:11, 'Ask the LORD your God for a sign, whether in the deepest depths or in the highest heights,'" I say, imitating my mother's Southern accent.

"How about we ask God to have our future husbands give us a gift? That way, when they give it to us, we'll know it's meant to be. It's like a stamp of approval, right? From the big man Himself." She wiggles her eyebrows.

"Tevah, that's not going to work."

"But what if it does work? It's in the Bible. It has to work, right? God is saying we can ask for whatever we want, no matter how big, no matter how small, feel me?"

"I don't know, Tevah." I watch tree after tree along the sidewalk as the radio plays the same damn rap song for the millionth time this week.

"I would ask God to have my husband present me with flowers... No, not flowers. That shit's too easy. What about honey-mustard pretzel pieces?"

I clear my throat. "You must be hungry?"

"Hell yeah, I'm hungry. I would have sex with honey-mustard pretzel pieces, but the shit might burn, feel me? So what would you want your future husband to give you, Sym?"

I squeeze my eyebrows. I try not to envision Tevah sticking a pretzel piece up her vagina and try to shake the image out my brain.

"Even though I'm almost positive I'm cursed, I'll humor you. How about a 1930s, fourteen-carat gold music box with a gold horse inside?" I say, playing her game.

She looks unimpressed.

"Hey, you asked? Oh, and it has to have my initials engraved and play a song I recognize," I say to make things more difficult.

"Sym, you don't know any songs from the 1930s!"

"Exactly."

"I'll be on my third marriage by the time you get all that!" Tevah says, laughing.

I shake my head. "If you're on your third marriage that means you're not waiting on those pretzel pieces to come. Don't make me laugh. I'm still mourning my love life. I hate this feeling." I spin my anxiety ring as I watch the trickle of rain stop.

We drive up the long, concrete road to the neighborhood called Mount Forty. The name comes from the twenty old, Victorian-style homes on both sides of the street. The only other way out is if you keep driving straight through. Mount Forty is a thousand feet high from the ground on the side of the I-5 freeway. It's the length of a football field with manicured lawns on the flat surface of a mountain. Its location is right outside of Sacramento, which is the place we refer to as "*The City*".

My father's construction company— which he took over from my grandpa—helped build this place way before I was born. Everybody knows each other, and a lot of the neighbors spend a lot of the time competing against each other.

Like Mrs. Wallace had her landscaper sculpt three panda bear faces out of her bushes on her front lawn. The next day, Ms. Evelyn next door had her landscaper make her a huge panda bear too, except her panda bear bush laid on his back playing with a massive bush ball. Dad thought it would be funny if he paid the landscaper to sculpt our bushes into a middle finger at the petty nonsense.

Especially after Ms. Wallace bought a state-of-the-art fountain with a panda bush on top. She put it right smack in the middle of her lawn, and at night, the blue illuminates behind the fountain water. My dad and Sheila's husband from across the street were the only two guys on the block. Mrs. Wallace had a husband too, but no one's ever seen him. Almost every house on Mount Forty has a bunch of middle-aged, single women with dogs who hump on trees or their owners. Oh, and they have funny-looking cats too.

One time, I caught a furless cat watching me outside my window with huge, wrinkly-egg eyes, and he watched me change out of my shirt. Pervert.

Back to what I was saying. The women on Mount Forty are vultures—always flirting with my dad. And they always tried to get him to come into their houses to fix something. But my dad would always send one of his workers over instead.

No wonder why mom doesn't attend the Friday night book club.

During the holiday's people come from far and wide to tour the neighborhood, especially around Christmas. People come to view the extravagant light shows and gigantic, custom reindeer on the front lawns, and that's a competition too.

I look up at our two-story brick house. My bedroom window is slightly open upstairs. Thank God. It can get blazing hot in my room.

There is a woman parked across the street, in front of Cash's mom's house, in a red Volkswagen Beetle. She has pale skin, long, black hair, and black shades. She's standing between the driver-side door with her hands in her brown trench coat. *But why is she staring at our house?*

Tevah turns the steering wheel and parks on the sloped driveway in front of the garage.

We're used to people coming to see the old Victorian-style homes during the Christmas season, but it's February, which makes this totally out of the ordinary.

Tevah says, "who is that?"

I say, "I remember that red buggy. I don't know

who she is, but I saw her last year from my bed-room window doing the same thing. Just standing and staring from across the street. Creepy." We've been parked a few seconds, and the lady hasn't budged. It's like she's in a daze or something.

Tevah hops out of the car, stands on the side-walk, and yells across the street. "Excuse me! Why are you staring at my house?"

Both hands shoot out her jacket pockets, star-tled. She quickly jumps into the red buggy and drives off in a hurry.

Tevah shrugs her shoulders and looks back at me. She says, "what the fuck was that about?"

I scratch the back of my head. "I have no idea." I stand between the passenger-side door with my elbows on the hood of the car.

She says, "that's weird."

My email notification rings, and I slide my fin-ger over the screen. *The Hollyview Network?* "We are excited to offer you the Celebrity News An-chor position with our company," I whisper and look at Tevah.

Our bubble-gum eyes pop open. On the verge of excitement, I pause when the notification bell rings again. It's from Professor Fenwal.

Tevah screams, "I'm so proud of you! Congratu-lations!"

I click on the email. It reads:

I'm sorry to inform you that you have failed the journalism final examination. As a result, you are re-quired to repeat this class.

Today couldn't get any worse. I melt into devastation and humiliation at the bottom of a bowl of failure. Not even getting the job offer could turn this day around. Especially because my future depends on passing that class. Anxiety pulls hard with each breath. I gasp.

"Tevah, I thought you talked to Professor Fenwal?" I mutter. Tevah walks around the car when she sees the look on my face and reads it. "Oh, shit! You didn't pass?" she asks.

A few months back, Tevah came to visit me at school. She stood at the door entrance waiting for me. Professor Fenwal's googly eyes stared at Tevah for so long they almost caused a scene. When I didn't pass the exam, I used that moment to my advantage and told Professor Fenwal Tevah was interested in him. Then, all of a sudden, he told me he made a mistake with the grading process and allowed me to retake the test the next day, but I didn't get my results until now. Tevah swore if I ever auctioned her off again, she would chop off my hair in my sleep. But after I showed her his social media photo, she was at a loss for words at how he hadn't reached thirty yet and thought his sexy, brown complexion was delicious, so she agreed to one date with him, even though he had baby-kangaroo hands.

Tevah says, "I had a date with Fenwal the other day, he didn't mention anything. Don't worry, Sym. You can take the class over this summer."

"Tevah, do you know what this means? The graduation ceremony is this summer, and the job offer is contingent on having a Bachelor's degree! If they find out I don't have a degree, they'll retract their offer and give it to someone else."

Before finals, I let Todd take me to Jamaica. Maybe not my best decision. I screwed up on a lot of tests by spending so much time with him. But I can't blame anybody but myself. I already have to fight to get any respect around here. The last thing I want to hear is what my parents have to say. I can hear Dad now.

"Baby Girl, if you're not responsible enough to do your schoolwork, I doubt you'll make it in the real world. Put down that chicken! And Mom. Bless your irresponsible heart. Why don't you stay home a little longer with me until you get your priorities straight?"

"I'm sorry, Sym," Tevah says with a frown.

"I'm never getting married. I hate Fridays. I hate school. I need my bed." I head toward the front door. I turn the key and push the door into the foyer. My knees turn to mush and both arms shoot out to steady my balance. "You have got to be kidding me!"

The twenty-foot banner hanging across the wooden balcony snatches my eyes. Written in pink and blue bold font, it reads, *"We Will Miss You, Sym!"*

Mariah Carey's song, *"Always Be My Baby"* bounces off the vaulted ceiling, and the smell of warm cinnamon enters my nostrils.

Tevah scans the room. "Mom didn't throw me a party when I left. Spoiled ass."

The pink and blue streamers swirl down the

wooden stairwell, colorful balloons cover most of the floor, and the sea of purple flowers on the wall still pisses me off every time I have to look at it. I kick the blue balloon, and it floats.

"Excuse me, ma'am," says the deep voice behind us as we stand at the door entrance.

There stands a guy with a green hat, brown hair, and a shirt that reads Photo Booth City.

"Hi! I'm here to drop off the photo booth. Can you sign here?" he says, putting the clipboard in front of me. I look at him like blue jelly is oozing out his eyeball.

Tevah grabs the pen. "I'll sign it!"

"Mom, where are you?" I shout, marching toward the kitchen.

THE FLOWERS
ON THE WALL

I **want to** *run back out the front door, but self-doubt holds me back like a prison guard. My reality is staring at me with a Rick James apron, folded butterscotch arms, and stands there like a blinking statue with dramatically concerned eyelashes.*

She's Elaine Dunmore, aka Mom, aka Laney. Her smile can make a blind man see, but she'd still pop him upside the head if he got out of line.

I eye her. So, Plan B it is. I had to stay and fight. I gave her the rundown of everything that just happened at Todd's place. She has this expression of worry, but what comes out her mouth isn't comforting at all.

"Bless your troubled heart. Symphony, I only invited a few people. Don't worry!" she says in her most sultry, Southern accent. My mother's voice is soft in manner, but she has a high-pitched tone like she's reading the church announcements on a microphone. I always have to remind her that I'm standing in front of her and not down the street. My plan was to go upstairs, mind my business, and be miserable behind closed doors. I don't want to be in this emotional state in front of the world. *You know what I mean?*

"Mom, thank you, but no thank you. I don't like surprises." I lean against the kitchen island.

She places one fist on the side of her thick diamond belt, and the flared-black dress shifts when she moves her voluptuous thighs. The knives on her sexy heels make a clunk as she shifts her feet. She always said, *"Women should always wear modest dresses, but the Lord didn't say anything about heels. Now that ain't in the Bible."*

Mom's holding a weapon, a broom.

"Symphony, you worked four years for your degree. Why wouldn't you want to celebrate?"

I throw out my palms, begging for her to understand. "Listen, I don't want to be bothered right now. Mom, cancel the party."

Her eyes grew wide as if I told her to kiss my ass. She shakes her head. Her perfectly cut bangs slightly move above her eyebrows, and a piece of her bob hairdo flips, but then falls back in place like nothing ever happened.

"I can't cancel at the last minute! Besides, you'll be abandoning your mother to fend for myself in this big ol' house! You need to be around family before you leave... girl, you gon' make my fibromyalgia flare up."

"It's not my fault you kicked Daddy out for no

reason. And you don't have fibromyalgia," I say, giving off the first shot in this war. *Bang, bang!*

My mother is so afraid of catching some type of disease that she diagnosed herself, not the doctor. She sucks in air, and her eyeballs scanned the room in a panic like she heard a noise. She puts her index finger in front of her mouth.

"Shush, Symphony. You shut your mouth, girl. Don't you know the Lord is listening? You do know it's a commandment to honor your father and mother, now don't you? It's in the Bible. You don't want your days cut short on this earth, now do you? Remember to fear God and keep His commandments."

Here she goes. My mother can be so dramatic, but she has the ability to stay so poised and full of grace, like she's too good to lose control. She's calm at times... but a little too calm to say the least. She curls her painted-red lips. She must have found some truth in my insult because she's pissed off. I don't know why... because she did kick Dad out for no reason.

"Not that it's your business, but I kicked your father out because he's a cheater! You hear me? A cheater he is, little girl! I'm giving you this dinner party whether you like it or not!"

"Mom, Daddy never cheated. It's all in your head just like the fibromyalgia diagnosis you gave yourself," I say under my breath. I fold my arms. Louder, I add, "Well, I won't be there!"

She points her finger with every word. "Symphony, I'm sorry your engagement ended so quickly with that foolish boy. But if you are missing in action tonight, it's going to take a special kind of surgeon to retrieve my Bible from your behind. Then I guess they'll give that job offer to somebody else, now won't they!"

"Woo," says Tevah, with a smirk on her face, standing in the kitchen entrance. She looks down at her shorts and pretends to wipe off an imaginary bug.

The stir of anxiety turns into a full-fledged tornado in my stomach. Facts are, they're going to give the job to somebody else anyway because I'm not graduating on time. *I had to tell Mom, but what could I say? I didn't study because I wanted to spend time with Todd. Remember him? The one with the prostitute? Nope, I can't do it. I can't tell her right now.*

Mom slides a purple mitten on her hand. She pulls the baked beans out of the oven, mumbling something under her breath about ungrateful children.

Yup, now she's mad, but is she mad enough to cancel the party? I spin the anxiety ring. Yup, that's what I need. A controlled rhythm. Yes. That's what I want. Control is what I need.

"Symphony, get the butter out of the refrigerator," she demands. I open the refrigerator and reach down to grab the butter from inside the door.

"Symphony, close the refrigerator. You're letting out the cold air," she snaps in frustration.

45

"Mom, I just opened it."

"Hush up. If your father was here, you wouldn't be talking back like this."

"But I wasn't—"

"I hung your party dress on the closet door. Go get your clothes on. You have a few hours before the guests arrive. And Tevah, stop actin' like you're not listening. Girl, ain't nothing on your shorts," Mom says, wiping the counter with a floral dish towel.

I guess I lost this war. But why does she treat me like I'm still a ten-year-old girl who needs help finding a training bra at Macy's? It's just not right. But I don't have to worry about it now because I'll be on a plane tomorrow, and there's nothing that's going to stop me. I've got at least six thousand in the bank to last me a good two months in L.A. with no job. I'll bus tables at the Piggly Wiggly for my half of the rent if I have to. I don't ever want to move back here. I sigh.

I say, " we're adults, remember? Don't you think we're a little too old for you to be picking out our party outfits?"

"I agree," says Tevah.

Mom stops wiping and passes us an inquisitive side-eye. "I got to work on that, but I ain't making no promises!" She looks back and forth at us with a get-out-my-face squint.

"Thank you," I say sarcastically as I walk away. I head up the dark, steep staircase. I have no choice but to endure the painful sight of millions of tiny purple flowers with a dreadful yellow background on the wall. My mom insists that we kept the house in its original state from when her grandfather owned it, no matter how hideous it looks. On the way up, I gaze down over the wooden rail at Grandma Bonnie's old room. Her door is slightly open. Nobody ever goes inside there except my father, from time to time, and my mother might go in there to dust. One time, my mother asked me to get the duster from the nightstand in there, but as soon as I stepped in, the coldness made the hairs on my arms stand.

Year One with Grandma Bonnie

Grandma Bonnie was the meanest woman I ever met. She had reddish skin, a round, yoga-ball belly, thick, ham-hock arms, and wore two silver French braids with a part down the middle of her head. She always had on a satin rose muumuu dress, which she never washed because it smelled like the public bathroom. Most grandmothers love and spoil their grandchildren, but Grandma Bonnie was the total opposite. She always had this disgusted look on her face every time Duck, Tevah, and I went to her house with Mom and Dad, which wasn't by choice. Grandma Bonnie's house smelled like old bananas, and she kept piles of clothes and mini-Christmas artifacts everywhere. Tevah, Duck, and I were too scared to sit down next to the clothes because we thought a creature might jump out and crawl on us, which meant we stood the entire visit.

"Tell those kids not to whisper in my house! Tell those kids not to look at me like that! Tell those kids not to touch my stuff!" Grandma Bonnie said through her congested accent.

She said, "Tell those kids" so much, I almost forgot we were related. My father was the only one in complete denial. Grandma Bonnie hated us.

"She's just an old woman. Don't take her too seriously," Dad would say. My father was the apple of Grandma's eye, but she treated everybody else like they didn't belong, including my mother. The story is, back in the sixties, grandpa divorced her and joined one of the black, Hebrew-Israelite organizations, which didn't allow interracial marriage. For years, Grandma Bonnie was a single mother, raising my dad and Tevah's biological father, so Grandma grew accustomed to them doing everything around the house. But they eventually moved out on their own. Dad married Mom and that's when Grandma treated my mother like she stole her man. So when Duck, Tevah, and I came along, we were an extension of my mother, which made us the enemy by default.

Dad would say, "Mother, say hi." Her nostrils would flare at me, Duck, Tevah, and my mother like we were stinky vinegar. Grandma Bonnie's carpet was a shaggy, dark-brown color. I remember thinking why would someone want boo-boo-colored carpet? Truth is, I hated bugs, so I was too scared that something might jump out and suck me back into the carpet, and I would never be found again.

Tevah would whisper, "why do we gotta take off our shoes in this nasty ass house?"

Duck would lift up his foot and examine the bottom of his white sock. He would say, "This carpet is getting my brand-new Nike socks dirty. Gorillas don't even live like this in the jungle."

Mom would sit there with a pretty smile, and sometimes she would clean up while Dad talked to Grandma in the Samoan language, but Dad was the only one who could understand. Grandma Bonnie never spoke to Mom directly.

She would look at Dad and say, "tell your wife not to touch my stuff. I like it right where it is!"

Now that she said in English. One day, Dad told us Grandma Bonnie had diabetes, which explained the twenty packs of unwrapped candy we saw on the kitchen floor. Dad couldn't take it anymore, seeing Grandma Bonnie living in filth, barely taking care of herself at eighty years old.

"Mother, I want you to move in with us," said Dad.

My mom would look at my dad like he left his mind in the car.

THREE HOURS
BEFORE THE PARTY

*O*ne tan heel *lands in front of the closet. The other bounces off the silver comforter on the bed. Finally, I'm alone. I shut the bedroom door behind me. I slip into my comfy Snoopy slippers and grab some licorice out of the plastic, cylinder container on the wooden dresser. The cranberry dress hangs on the closet door. It's strapless with sequins and lace with a sweetheart neckline. At least, Mom has good taste in clothes. My tank top and jeans land behind the hamper. I throw on a SUPER BESHIE T-shirt and lean back on the bed. I stick my earbuds in my ears, press play on my phone, and close my eyes. The soulful songstress is singing about how somebody took her man. An escort took mine... What a damn shame. I guess I'm not the only one with man problems.*

"I can't believe she took my man..." sings in my ear by Tamar Braxton. If I learned anything from this breakup, it was that I dodged an Uzi gun of deceitful bullets. What if I found out all his dirty habits after I married him? Thank you, God.

Something warm touches my arm. My stomach leaps, and my pulse races around the track.

"Tevah, are you trying to kill me?" I shout, holding my hand over my chest.

Her mouth is moving, but no words come out. I pull the earbuds.

I sit up and gasp. "What?"

"He's coming!" she says.

"Who?" I look around for a hairy, red monster.

"Professor Fenwal's coming to the party!"

I squint in confusion. "Why is Professor Fenwal coming to this house?" I point to the floor for emphasis.

"I told him we were having a going-away party for you, and he insisted on coming. Plus, he wants to see me, of course," she says, smacking her lips in arrogance.

"How unthoughtful of you, Tevah. You invite him to invade my space and chow down on my party food after he failed me in his class? Fenwal is a freaking savage!" I shake my head in defeat.

"Shit, my bad. Maybe things can turn around. I don't know, but I'll see you downstairs. Cute dress. I have the same one in black." She shuts the door behind her.

Is this some kind of sick joke?

I tilt my head back, and my eyes look up. I put both hands together, and my fingertips point to the ceiling.

"God," I pray, "can you miraculously change my journalism grade so I can graduate on time? Can we work out a deal or something? I know it's cheating, but I did study real hard when I took the test over. I didn't believe in signs before, but if you do me this favor, I promise not to have sex or marry until you send me a sign from my future husband. I want the man I'm supposed to marry to give me a 1930's gold music box with a gold horse inside. Oh, and it has to play a song I recognize and have my initials engraved."

The water in my eyes blurs my vision.

"Please do me this favor. In Your name, Jesus, I pray. Amen."

Both hands fall to the mattress in defeat. What's done is a wrap that can't unfold.

Why did I put myself in this situation? I swallow.

I use the back of my hand to wipe away the wetness.

❉ ❉ ❉

I could really use a chocolate milkshake right now to calm my salty nerves. Why would Tevah set me up like this? Professor Fenwal is going to shut this entire party down. He's going to shout to the world how bad I did in his class. Then I will spend the rest of the night explaining how I screwed up. My eyelids flutter—there it is. There's stress coming to play with my emotions. I open the door, and the savory aroma is so delicious I can taste the coconut on my tongue.

"Yummy, Pani Popo." The freshness of coconut bread forces my stomach to purr in delight.

I look over the wooden balcony. Doesn't look like anyone's here yet.

The blasting music turns off as I walk downstairs.

"What's wrong, Laney?" The deep voice in the kitchen sounds familiar. I stay in the dining room and peek around the wall. Mom pours a bunch of corn in the pot. There he is—six feet five inches of Mr. Thomas Dunmore, aka Tommy, aka *my father*, standing across the kitchen island with love and concern in his eyes.

They met and fell in love thirty-something years ago at the Sacramento Airport only two days after Dad started working there to get some extra cash. At that point, he was in his late teens and didn't know if he wanted to take over the construction business from his father. Mom flew in from her hometown of Memphis, Tennessee. Dad helped with her luggage and never left her side. Well, until she kicked his ass out a few years back.

The light reflects off his shiny, bald, apricot head. His eyebrows look permanently annoyed, but he's the epitome of why people shouldn't judge a book by its cover. Yes, he has a teardrop tattoo near his eye, but he didn't kill anybody. His friend dared him to tattoo his face back in the early nineties. Even though Dad has the appearance of a man who has a criminal record as long as California, he's the most loving father any girl could ever ask for. Sure, he's rough around the edges and socially awkward at times, but he adores my mother. It's sort of funny though how strangers stop and ask Mom indirectly if she's being held against her will, insinuating my dad kidnapped her because of how mean-looking and huge he is, but what they don't know is, even though my mother may appear nice and sweet, she's the reason why my dad has a permanent limp when he walks.

"C'mon, Laney, what's wrong?" Dad asks with his baritone just above a whisper. Mom's head hangs low. I wonder if I put her in a bad mood.

"Tommy, I'm fine."

Dad wipes his short, garlic-and-pepper goatee.

"Thirty years of marriage... I know when something's up. Is it Symphony? She'll come back to visit just like Tevah does. I'm sure of it." Dad rubs his hand over the tribal tattoos on his neck, and his unbuttoned palm shirt shows other tattoos with intricate lines. Dad always wore some type of tropical shirt whether we celebrated a birthday, Tequila Festival, or Kwanzaa.

"Tommy, I'm worried about Symphony. She broke things off with that boy before she could even get into planning her wedding good," says Mom.

"Good. I didn't like the fucker, anyway! What kind of man doesn't ask the father for his approval to marry his daughter?" He places his hand on his round beer belly, but his arms are massive and strong enough to build a house.

"I didn't like him, either," Mom says.

Wow, so this is what they think? Maybe that snot-cry at the wedding dress boutique didn't mean she was happy.

"Tommy, how'd you get in the house?" asks Mom.

"This is still my house, Laney. Don't start! I used my key," Dad says.

"Well, I thought you gave it back. You been knocking every time you come around. What's different about today?" she says.

"I'm here to celebrate with my baby girl! I don't have time for this nonsense."

"Well, don't be surprised when your keys don't work next time," she says, raising an eyebrow.

"Laney, if you don't want me using my key, I won't use it then!" The side of his fist pounds on the marble countertop.

Mom looks at his massive fist like it belongs to a toddler throwing a tantrum. Unfazed, she turns around and pours the leftover peas in the sink. She flicks on the garbage disposal, and it doesn't growl. She sighs.

"I'll fix it. I just got to go get my tools from the car," says Dad.

"You have been saying that for two weeks now. Should I call someone else to fix it?"

"No, Elaine! I'll fix it." Dad never calls Mom by her government name. He must be really frustrated. She turns off the pot of rice.

"Come on, Laney. Don't be like that. I'm here to celebrate my baby girl. She's about to graduate and start a new life in a new place. How can you still be this angry after three years? Damnit,

Laney!" He reaches in his back pocket, pulls out a white handkerchief, and wipes the sweat from his forehead.

He has got to stop calling me baby girl. I'm not a baby anymore. I can see my baby sonogram on his forearm. That's me, his sweet baby girl. The sonogram is partly why they think I'm so spoiled around here. Although Dad has all these tattoos, he never managed to put Duck or Tevah's sonogram on him, even though he promised he would.

Mom's sweet potato pie is right there on the counter! I would punch somebody to taste it right now. But the last thing I want to hear is my father's voice.

"Baby girl, you sure you need a slice of pie?" he would say. I would usually smile on the outside but shrink on the inside. I guess smiling is my defense mechanism to make the moment less awkward. I guess to make everyone else around the room comfortable at my expense. As many times that I've pleaded with Dad to stop bringing up how heavy I used to be, he brushes it off and says, *"We Dunmores aren't sensitive people."* The most frustrating part was he acted like I wasn't responsible enough to maintain my own weight. Never mind the fact that I worked the weight off without his help. It was like he picked a wound that healed a long time ago. This is another reason why I absolutely can't wait to leave tomorrow.

Mom looks up at Dad with a curious expression. "Tommy, how old is that girl you're bringing here?" says Mom.

"Twenty-nine, why?"

"What would she think about you rubbing your johnson up against my behind a while ago?" says Mom.

If I vomit, will it blow my cover? My father has completely lost his mind. *What was he thinking inviting his new girlfriend over?* Didn't he just meet her? Did Mom actually have a problem with it? If I knew my father, he had a good comeback line to Mom's question.

"What I do with my wife is my business," he says, stomping one foot.

"Oh, really?" Her head jerks back, and she raises her eyebrows in amazement.

"Well, guess what... Your wife contacted a divorce attorney, and your wife's new boyfriend, Steve, is on his way." She pours in the soy sauce, chives, sugar, garlic, and ginger for the Shoyu chicken.

It's always nice to have a mixture of soul food and island food. Has Daddy ever heard to never piss off the cook? Wait... Did Mom say boyfriend? Dad is watching her, but his chest isn't moving.

I remember the last time Dad pissed Mom off. That day, I spent at least an hour in the shower conditioning my hair. I stepped out of the bathroom and saw Mom stuff Dad's palm-tree shirts and khaki pants into a white grocery bag. She tied the plastic handles, glided to the balcony, and tossed the full bag over the balcony. The massive plop echoed through the house. I looked over the balcony and saw at least two dozen stuffed and tied bags stacked like a mountain in the middle of the foyer downstairs.

"Mom, did you throw all these?" I asked. Her eyes reminded me of a new security guard clutching her gun, itching for a reason to shoot.

"Help me take these bags outside," Mom said. At that point, I didn't feel like I had a choice. Dad parked across the street in his white construction truck at the exact moment I walked out the front door holding the last stuffed grocery bag. He got out, slammed the truck door, and stopped mid-street with his mouth wide open like he caught a robber walking out the front door with his television. Except it wasn't a robber. It was me holding the last bag of his belongings to put on the curb with the other bags. Talk about the most awkward moment ever. I don't know what my father did, but I'd sure hate to be him. I handed him the bag.

"Is your mother upset with me?" That was the first time I saw fear in my father's eyes.

I gave him a swift, "Yup." Before I headed back to the porch, I couldn't figure out why Mom parked her silver Camry in front of the next-door neighbor's house. But when I looked straight ahead, Mom was standing in the doorway with no expression. It was like watching a silent movie.

My father walked back and forth, loading his stuff in the back of the truck. Mom nudged me as she headed to the sidewalk, clutching a white piece of paper.

She walked up to Dad and slammed the paper flat on his face. He grabbed the paper and viewed it, and his expression morphed from offended to terror. Mom snatched back the paper, crumpled it into a ball, and headed in the direction of her silver Camry. Mom started the engine, and the car sped straight in Dad's direction.

"Daddy, watch out!" The car nicked the side of his right leg, knocking all two hundred seventy-five pounds of my father to the concrete next to the grocery bags. What scared me wasn't the fact that she hit my father with her car. It was her ability to stay incredibly calm that terrified me. Like she could go right back in the house to finish the laundry like nothing ever happened. Mom backed up the car. I ran in front of Dad as he got up slow, and the car screeched and stopped two inches in front of my outstretched palms. I'm pretty sure I forgot to breathe.

Mom slowly backed up, made sure not to hit the green trash can, and slowly parked in our driveway. I swallowed hard. She carefully climbed out of the car, walked back to the house, and the stained-glass shattered when she slammed the door. I helped throw the rest of the grocery bags in the back of his truck as he limped back and forth. I knew I couldn't let Dad stay too much longer because I didn't know what Mom might do next. My dad owned a lot of guns, and they were in the house with Mom. Disappointment beamed from his face.

"Your mother would believe anything. Even if it ain't true," he said before he kissed me on the cheek. He limped to his truck, got in, and drove off with no further explanation. Luckily, the neighbors weren't *around to call the police. That day, I made the craziest decision I'd ever made in my life. I passed on UCL.A. and chose to stay at my parents' house and attended Sacramento State College in the city. I didn't want my mom going to prison for murdering my dad for whatever they had going on.*

I don't know what evidence Mom had when she referred to him as a cheater earlier. I don't think he would ever do something like that. It's been a few years since that happened, and at this point, I'm dealing with a father who made it his job to remind me of how overweight I used to be, and a mom who still invades my privacy by coming in my room without permission to wash my clothes, including my damn underwear. *I'm so, so serious. She does.* So I'm not letting anything or anybody stand in my way this time. I'm moving to L.A., and I don't care if Mom has Dad and his new girlfriend tied up butt naked on the dining room table. I'm leaving tomorrow, and I might not come back.

"Boyfriend?" Dad says, eyes wide.

He heard her right. Mom has got a boyfriend. This is my cue to leave. I couldn't listen anymore. Professor Fenwal is about to devastate my entire existence when he gets here, and I don't know how I'm going to explain failing my class to my parents. I head back upstairs. My parents are still crazy about each other. *Why can't they see that?*

TWO HOURS BEFORE THE PARTY

I **shut the** *door behind me. I was so close to getting the job, and I blew it. But I'll practice anyway. I stare intensely at the brown eyes in the mirror. I pick up the leopard pen off the dresser and wrap my fist around it like it's a microphone. High energy this time, Sym.*

"Hi! I'm Sym Dunmore coming at you live, and guess what... I'm ready to give you the hottest celebrity news right here on the Hollyview Network!"

No, Sym. You can do better. Jump out the safe box. You can do it.

As a kid, I loved being on camera. Having my mother's attention meant everything to me. Dad ran the construction business while Mom spent a lot of time cooking, cleaning, and taking care of us. I would sing a radio song, dance, or merely have an entire conversation while she recorded me on her cell phone with a smile on her face. She looked at me like I was a shining star. There's something about being on cam-

era that makes me feel heard… like I have the attention of the world. Being the youngest, sometimes it's like I'm speaking an unfamiliar language because they pretend not to understand or don't take my words seriously, so talking into a camera makes me feel like they have no choice but to listen to what I have to say.

I'm not the baby of the family anymore. I'm all grown up. I can't lie, though. Stepping out into a new place like Los Angeles scares me. Meeting new people in a new environment sends chills down my back. But like my mother used to say, people bleed just like you do, so if anything, picture everybody naked with watermelon heads to help break the ice. I clear my throat. *"Hi! My name is Sym Dunmore, and I'm here to give you the latest celebrity news, but first, a public service announcement. If you can't be yourself around him, move on to the next man who loves you for who you are…"*

The thumping police knock made me drop the leopard pen. "Mom, are you serious?" I say while opening the door.

My eyes light up in shock. A husky guy with a short beard and curly, black hair is staring at me with a grin on his apricot face.

"What's up, dude. Mom never threw me a party. Spoiled ass," says my big brother, Duck, with both hands inside his pockets. He's the only person in the world I'd ever let call me dude. He used to say it's because he always wanted a little brother, but it turns out, Mom and Dad thought they were having a boy right before I was born.

"Duck!" I scream. He catches me in the air, and I wrap my arms around his shoulders. He swings me around in excitement as we laugh. I haven't seen my big brother in three months. He's four years older and recently enlisted in the army.

One day, he was a guidance counselor for the Sacramento School District. Next minute, he sat us all down with Tevah via FaceTime in L.A. and told us he enlisted in the army. The next day, he left his apartment and flew to Texas for training camp for the US Army. It's three months later, and he's back? Before he left, he snuck into my room and hid a pile of dog shit under my bed, and he strategically placed it on a square, white napkin. Crazy thing was we didn't even have a dog! It took me three days to get that smell out of my room. He's one of the reasons why I want to get my own place! At least I'll have control over who's allowed in my room. I remembered when Duck Saran wrapped the toilet. Totally not cool waking up in the middle of the night to have pee splattered everywhere!

Duck puts me down, and we do our special handshake: front clap, back clap, shoulder bounce twice, "dab on them" arms, and dab once again.

I say, "Duck, why aren't you in training camp? I'm confused."

Duck runs his hands over his short hair. He looks good enough for the red carpet in his exquisitely tailored suit. Duck is more of a shorter version of my dad but with hair.

He rubs his bumpy, snub nose. He says, "Dude, they sent me back early."

"Why would they do that?"

"Well, I submitted a request. Plus, my paperwork got mixed up, so I'm here until they figure it out."

"Well, I guess you came on a good day. We're having a party," I say sarcastically. His eyes are so round and eager to tell me something new. My brother's more of a computer nerd, always ready to tell me something new he found on the World Wide Web.

"I got back in town yesterday. I told Mom I wanted to surprise you."

His real name is Patrick Dunmore, but we call him Duck. He inherited the nickname when we were kids because he was the only one who ducked down low when Mom used to throw stuff at us. Mom's way of disciplining us consisted of throwing whatever she saw to teach us a lesson. Shoes, dish towels, books, she didn't discriminate. But my brother always managed to dodge whatever she threw, but Tevah and I weren't so lucky. So we call him Duck. Funny thing is after Mom threw around something, she would gracefully turn around and watch television like she didn't care, like throwing stuff at us was part of her job as a mother.

Duck says, "Dude, congrats on your degree!" His chipper voice drags out the word degree.

Those words took a chunk out of my pride. I want to forget about my problems, but I'm sure graduation will come up at least fifty times tonight. He wouldn't be so proud if he knew how much of a failure I am.

I can't tell him. I'm not ready. The shock consumes me. I'm not graduating on time, is what I want to say, but I can't. Not after all the guys he beat up on my behalf. Back in high school, there was always at least one guy who thought thicker girls didn't have the right to love themselves, so they would say rude comments, like calling me the chunky girl with the pretty face, but when my brother found out about what happened back then, he would go up to the school and slap the guys around as if they owed him rent money.

I say, "thanks, Duck. I worked really hard for that degree. I can't wait to be out there on my own, you know, because I'm a grown woman, I need my space!"

"Here you go... 'I'm a big girl now!' Yeah, yeah, I get it!" he teases in a little girl voice.

My brother is certainly a happy-go-lucky kind of guy, but when it comes to me, he's protective... a little too protective. Maybe I can get him to pay Todd's cheating ass a visit. The thought forms a smile on my face.

A guy leans against the frame of the door. He has hot mocha skin and narrow nostrils that come to a pointed tip. He rubs his five-o'clock shadow and stings me with his sharp, exhilaratingly sexy, brown eyes. I guess he got rid of those prescription glasses. He has faded hair, and his sex appeal in that tuxedo is at 20,000 watts. I sigh, not because he looks like a tasty fudge brownie and not because he broke my soul five years ago, but because he's my best friend.

"Cash?" I say in a weak voice.

SUIT AND TIE

I **remember standing** *in front of John F. Kennedy High School waiting on Duck to pick me up, and he was late as usual. But at least it was sunny this time. Charlie Brooker, a walking toothpick, ambled toward me, fidgeting with his hands. Weird guy. Back then, he was the only kid I saw with a buff frog tattoo on his twig arm. He always kept one side of this short sleeve rolled up to show it off too. He stood next to me. Five awkward seconds flew by before he opened his mouth.*

"Hey, Sym, do you think Ms. McCain's boyfriend really had sex with the lunch lady?" he asked. We had most of the same classes for four years. He's never spoken to me, and this is what he chose to ask me? And he's calling me Sym like we're close enough for him to shorten my name, like we've been friends our entire lives.

I said, "I'm seventeen. I shouldn't be giving relationship advice to a forty-five-year-old English teacher." I tugged on the strap of my purple backpack.

He jerked his head a little, and the red hair fell over his forehead, probably to hide the massive blood-red pimple. He looks at my stomach. "Wow, you're chub-

bier than I expected," he said.

"What?" I took a step back. His eyes shot open. And the crowd of students nearby snickered. Clearly, he confused his thoughts with what came out of his mouth.

"I'm sorry. It came out wrong! I mean, I like chunky girls. I mean, freckles are cool too. You're pretty though, I mean... How about I shut up?" He tightened his lips, gawking at the ground in embarrassment.

I thought after last year, I would not have to deal with this again. I didn't know whether to slap him or punch him, so I pointed my finger in his face.

"Listen, you pimple-faced idiot..."

An engine growled, making us jolt back. An apple-red Mustang growled to a stop beside us. Duck jumped out the driver side, grabbed Charlie by the shirt, and threw him against the side of the car.

My brother, here to save the day again, but I didn't need his help because I had things under control.

"Duck, stop!" I yelled.

"If I ever catch you around my sister, I'll cut that gigantic pimple off your forehead!"

Everyone laughed nearby.

"She has a security guard," said one of the guys in the crowd.

But somebody enjoyed this scene a little more than everyone else. My brother's friend, Cash, sat on the passenger side with a huge grin on his face. Cash Anderson. Voted the sexiest man on campus three years in a row on social media. Everyone thought he was on his way to the NFL to play football, but after he graduated, he quit. I blasted him with threatening eyes. He adjusted his prescription glasses and opened the door.

"Duck, get off him, man!" Cash grabbed Duck by the shirt and arm.

"Let's go, Sym! Dude, come on!" Duck demanded.

I climbed in the back seat and watched Charlie try to wipe off the tire dirt from his khaki shorts. It took me three times before I could get the seat belt over my stomach, and then I violently crossed my arms. Thanks to guys like Charlie, I had to fight even harder to convince my brother that I could defend myself. It was always that one guy who referred to my weight in a negative manner. I loved my body, so I never really got the idea of it all. Did they want a snack-sized dick metal? Or maybe the goal was to make me feel bad about being myself?

"Duck, why would you embarrass me like that?" I yelled.

"Dude, your finger was in his face! I thought he was trying to pick on you. He could've been a murderer or a sex lord in training... Do you think I'm going to let some guy pick on my baby sister? Ronnie, you don't fuckin' get it!" He slams the side of his fist on the dashboard.

"Calm down, man," said Cash.

"Ronnie? Who is Ronnie?" I asked.

"That's not what I meant to say." My brother had a way of making me feel defenseless, belittled, and disrespected, and now, he's so mad that he's calling me somebody else? Ronnie? Who is that?

"Sex lord?! Duck, I could've handled him myself!

I'm not a freaking baby anymore! And why would you think he was picking on me?"

"Well, it's my job to protect you, even though you don't think you need protection. Was he picking on you?" he asked.

I rolled my furious eyes when he gazed back at me.

"That's what I thought," he said with validation.

I twisted my knees to the side and stared out the window. Duck pushed in a CD and pulled over into the Bel-Air parking lot.

"I be on my suit-and-tie shit, tie shit..." played loudly through the speakers. Not fair. I loved Justin Timberlake, and he knew it. Duck sang the first verse, staring at me, and pretending to be Justin Timberlake.

Cash rocked side to side. He playfully lifted his eyebrows with emotion as they both exaggerated, singing the verse as if they performed in a concert. So I look out the window so they don't get the satisfaction of my attention. I don't know what it was, but I couldn't stop my head from moving to the music. And my finger had a mind of its own, tapping on the thigh of my blue skirt. Sixty seconds passed before the music possessed my body, and I exaggerated singing with them. Who could resist Justin Timberlake? I guess this was Duck's way of apologizing. And it clearly worked. He backed out of the parking spot and headed home. Cash's eyes caught mine in the passenger-side mirror. We were unapologetically in love, and my brother had no idea. That night, Cash snuck in my room. I lifted my Snoopy cover, and he laid down next to me.

"You know if my brother or dad caught you in

here, they'd leave your body on the grass across the street for your mom to find," I said, blinking in the dark.

"Your brother's in his bedroom snoring with his mouth open, and the PlayStation controller is still in his hand. But if I die loving you, I'll be alright. I got you something," he said anxiously.

"You did? What did you get me?"

He stuck his hand behind his back.

He turned the light on from his phone and shone it on something. It was a white, stuffed animal—a dog with a pink dress and bow on the top of her head.

"Snoopy's sister Belle? I love it, Cash," I muttered.

"I love you, Symphony Dunmore. Shit, you looked so beautiful today in that skirt."

Cash made me feel like the prettiest girl on the planet, and he hated when I wore extra-big T-shirts and oversized jeans to cover my meaty legs. He loved every part of me. He was the first guy to make me feel that way.

"I love you more, Cash Anderson. What are we going to do? You saw what my brother did to that guy today, and I barely knew the guy," I said.

"Sym, I'm going to tell your brother about us tomorrow. I'm going to tell him I love you," he said with eagerness in his deep tone.

"You promise?"

"I promise." He reached in and pressed his cushion lips on mine, then pulled back to see my reaction.

"I've never kissed a guy before. Well, not with tongue," I whispered.

He leaned over me and entered his mango-smooth tongue in my mouth and inhaled all of me with his minty-flavored kisses. My insides pulsated, and his heated energy absorbed my spirit. His hand slid between my thighs, then stopped.

"Why'd you stop?" I asked. "Are you ready?"

"Cash, I want you to be my first."

"Are you sure? I don't want to pressure you," he said.

I rubbed my hand on his chest. "I'm seventeen now. I've thought this through for six months now. Is something wrong?"

"Yeah. I'm nineteen. I could go to jail, I think."

"Cash, I want to." I slowly moved his hand up my thigh.

He gently tugged on my underwear, and then the security light from across the street shone through the window, blinding us for a second.

"Shoot, I forgot to close the curtains. Must have been the cat next door," I said as we snickered. The whites in his panicking eyes grew when the toilet flushed from down the hall.

"Oh my God! Get out of here before my father kills you. You won't be able to tell Duck tomorrow if you're dead," I whispered. I didn't hear any gunshots when he snuck out, so I assumed he made it back to Duck's room down the hall. The next morning, I saw Duck sitting on the couch watching television. I could see my mom and dad through the sliding door window, talking by the BBQ pit in the backyard. Duck looked a little too happy watching football. Clearly, Cash hadn't told *him yet.*

"Hey, Duck. Oh, did Cash go home already?"

"What's up, Dude... yeah. His uncle popped up and offered to let him stay with him in New York until he got his music producing career going."

"Yeah right, Duck." I laughed. I opened the front door and stood on the porch. Cash was sticking his luggage in the back of a black Toyota. My heart fell on an invisible sword. He saw me and hesitantly waved.

His lips formed the words, "I'm sorry."

I hated those two words ever since.

ONE HOUR BEFORE
THE PARTY

I can't believe Cash is standing in my doorway right now. This morning, he sent me a text message saying he was in Japan making music for a new recording artist. Cash is a super-music producer out in Los Angeles now. He makes music for a lot of celebrities. After Cash skipped town on me, he called two annoyingly long years later and apologized. We somehow managed to put the past behind and developed a close friendship. But I still never unblocked him from my social media accounts. It's been five years since I've laid eyes on him, and I must say I'm impressed.

"Duck, you didn't tell me your friend was here," I say, surprised. I walk in front of Cash. "Hi, Cash." I squeeze my fingers into a fist, and he fist bumps me back with his thick fingers. "Where are your glasses?" I ask.

He laughs. "I got Lasik treatments. You sure have grown," he says, observing me from head to thighs.

"Yup. I'm a woman now." He has a long object in his other hand.

"What do you have there?" I lean forward to grab it.

"I bought you a bottle of Gold Bubbles champagne," he says. The yellowish champagne can be seen through the gold-plated circles all over the bottle from top to bottom.

"Isn't Gold Bubbles $1,500 a bottle?" I stick my neck out.

He shows his incredibly straight, white veneers in humility. He reaches behind the wall and hands me a dozen pink balloons floating with colorful strings held down by a mini star weight playing twinkle little star music.

"It plays music when you move it unless you turn it off at the bottom," says Cash.

"Thanks, Cash." I put the balloons on the side of the dresser. When I let go of them, the music stopped. Cash gives me a squint with flirtation in his chocolaty eyes. He looks at my T-shirt, then wipes his mouth with the back of his hand. *I don't know what he's thinking, but if it's what I think it is, he should give up now. After the disaster I had today at Todd's house, all men are officially on my hate list. I repeat, all men.*

Cash scratches his hairy chin. "I bought a few more bottles, they're on the dining table downstairs. You deserve it, Ms. Dunmore." I give him a quick, awkward hug, and my brother is watching our every move.

Cash's charming demeanor comes off as flirtation. Hmm. Maybe I'm reading him wrong. "Thanks,

Cash!" I observe the gold bottle and set it on the dresser. "Wow. Twenty-eight percent alcohol content? A teaspoon of this would have me wobbling in my heels!" I exclaim.

My mind flashes back. *At the last party, I went to, I consumed just two shots of vodka, and Tevah found me in a dry bathtub asleep, using a blue towel as a blanket.*

"So are you ready for L.A.?" asks Duck while checking out the items on the dresser.

He better not...

"Yup. I'm so ready to leave this place," I say, watching Duck take the lid off the plastic container of my licorice candy. Before he can dig his hands in, I yell, "Stop!"

I open my drawer, grab the sanitizer, and squirt two pumps in his hands and mine. I hate germs. This side of me comes from my mom. Duck grabs a few Red Vines from the plastic jar.

There he goes again. Cash is playing with his tongue inside his cheek, and he's looking at my breasts. Duck turns toward Cash, and he straightens his shoulders, clears his throat, and admires my room like it's the most fascinating museum on earth. Should I tell him about what happened with Todd today? Maybe I shouldn't.

"Duck, is Chelsea downstairs?" I ask.

"No, she had to work." He scratches his arm.

Cash makes a noise with his throat. Why are men in this family such bad liars? I gave Duck a vicious squint while flinging the licorice from side to side in front of his face.

"What happened? Tell me, and I'll give you another one." He snatches the licorice out of my hand.

"We broke up, dude. Fuck, the sweet potato pie smells good downstairs," he says, chewing dramatically and sucking his teeth.

"Duck, don't think that changing the subject to sweet potato pie is going to distract me from the Chelsea question. And all you're going to do is stuff yourself, then snore like you do at every party." I look up at him with my palms on his shoulders.

"Did Chelsea find out about the other two women you proposed to last year?" I ask.

I don't think Duck has had a serious relationship that's lasted past six months. Like ever.

"What did you do this time? Put a tracker on her car?" I giggle. "Georgia made that shit up, dude!"

"Let me guess, you caught her with a guy, beat him up, and it turned out to be her cousin?"

"Dude, I'm telling you, Sym. You can't believe what you hear!" says Duck. Cash laughs, probably because he knows I'm right.

"I can help you with the ladies, bro. It's probably harder to date now that you're in the army though," I say.

"No, I'm fine. I just hooked up with a girl in the back of Taco Bell before I got here." He puts two fingers near my nose. "See? Smell it!"

I punch him on the arm.

"You're disgusting!" I shout.

"Come on. You won't catch anything! You do know that boogers in your nose are there to catch diseases, right?" Cash and I burst out in laughter.

Cash clears his throat. "That's tough. So boogers are stopping STDs now, bro? Where do you get this information?" Cash says, trying to catch his breath.

"Because I read, man!" says Duck like he's onto some government conspiracy. I raise my hand.

"Umm... Just so I don't have to talk about it later, it's over between Todd and me. Please don't ask why," I say, rubbing my fingertips on my forehead.

"Dude, I thought I told you to stay away from that guy. Shit, now I owe Dad ten dollars. Let me guess, he had another girl?" Duck says, gawking at me.

"Well..." I shrug.

"That's what I thought," he says, assuming the rest of my story. Cash shakes his head in pity.

Duck used to have a strained relationship with Dad, especially in his teenage years. So it's good they're communicating, even though they bet money on the downfall of my relationship. Duck is just like my dad personality wise. They can be so grumpy and so damn bossy but so loving at the same time.

I remember when Duck was sixteen. He got in an argument with Dad, marched upstairs, and slammed his bedroom door. Tevah turned off the show on the television we were watching, and we listened carefully, wondering what would happen next. I anticipated Dad would probably knock Duck's lights out. A few minutes later, we heard the loud vibration of a drilling tool. Then Dad hauled Duck's entire bedroom door down the stairs, mumbling, "You won't slam or punch another door in my muthafucking house, ever." Tevah and I laughed for two days. Every time we walked past Duck's bedroom, we made funny faces or pretended to knock on the invisible door. He threw pillows at us and threatened us, of course.

"Duck, I'd be in a convent somewhere wearing a black-and-white robe if I let you pick a guy for me." He wrestles with his curly hair.

"Doesn't sound like a bad idea." Duck and Cash laughs like it's the funniest thing ever. I point my finger in Duck's face. "And if you give Dad ten dollars for that stupid bet, I'll tell Dad you had sex in his bed in the twelfth grade. Yup, I remember. It was Jenny Johnson." I fold my arms.

"Dude, alright! You win!" says Duck.

Duck never liked any of the guys I've tried to date. He swears every guy in the world conspires against me. For what reason, I have no idea. He will always treat me like his baby sister, even when I'm fifty years old. Cash is in a daze, tugging at the diamond stud in his earlobe. There he goes, staring at my T-shirt.

"Alright, you win, but you need to know that these guys are monsters out here, and all they want to do is the humpty-hump, but as soon as they get the pum-pum, they're onto the next piece of ass."

Cash shakes his head in disagreement. "That's tough, but that doesn't apply to all men though. And you gotta stop watching those reality shows. Men don't say pum-pum!"

Now, I'm amused.

Duck passes Cash a "shut up" look.

Here's the moment when Duck starts sounding like Dad. I start pushing him toward the hallway.

"Well, thanks for coming. I got to get my clothes on for my party. And Duck, don't fall asleep after you eat!"

Duck shouts, "Men are animals! Don't trust them! It's okay. I'll be back. I'm about to do my part in society and consume some pie!"

"See you guys in a little bit, and Duck, turn on the music when you get downstairs!" They walk down the stairs, and I see Cash look back like he wants to munch on me for dinner.

"Stay away from my sister, man. She's not one of your groupies."

Cash looks at Duck in disgust. "What? That's tough. You know she's like a little sister to me."

"Yeah right... *sister*," says Duck, looking suspicious.

I shut the door. What was that about? The coldness is sharp through my T-shirt, and it shocks my back on the door. Me and Cash? Could we? After what he did to me? Absolutely not.

❋ ❋ ❋

It's been fifteen minutes since I kicked Duck out my room. I can hear Mariah Carey's music blasting downstairs. I lay my cranberry dress on the bed. A faint knock grabs my attention.

"Duck, I can date whoever I want!" I swing the door open. Cash stands there with a stupid smirk on his face holding a box the size of a bowling ball. It's wrapped in Snoopy gift paper.

"Congratulations, Symphony Dunmore."

"Cash, what are you doing?" I look left and right down the hall. I grab his rock hard arms and pull him into my room. "Does my brother know you're up here?" I say, eyes wide.

"Your dad started telling him about one of his old boxing stories, so I snuck off."

"Sym, you look amazing. I'm still shocked. How did you lose all the weight? I mean, you were beautiful the last time I saw you, but wow! You look even better!" I cross my arms.

"Thanks, Cash. It wasn't easy."

I want to break down and tell him everything that happened today with the escort and Professor Fenwal, but falling apart before my own party isn't a good idea.

He gives me the box, and I immediately tear off a piece of the wrapping paper.

"No, wait! I want you to open it later when we have a little more time. It's getting crowded downstairs. How about we meet back in your room at midnight?" he suggests.

Is he coming on to me right now? I'm so confused.

"Cash, I have to ask you something. Is this gift from a friend who happens to be my best friend or a gift from a guy who likes me?"

He looks down at the floor like he's thinking of what to say. "I haven't seen you in five years, and you fist bumped me earlier?"

Why is he ignoring my question? He wraps his rough fingers around my wrist, and a tingle shoots up my arm and travels inside my body. He pulls me toward him and wraps his strong arms around my waist, pulling me even closer. I softly inhale. The bold, provocative masculinity with a mixture of woods and citrus oranges is enough sweetness to make me want to take off my clothes... just like in the commercials.

"I need a proper hug," he says. I stand on my tippy-toes, wrapping my arms around his broad shoulders, and he slowly squeezes me tighter around my back, lifting all five feet and five inches of me effortlessly off the ground at eye level. Funny, my legs are dangling. We smile at each other in silence. I love everything about this moment, almost like we were meant to be here, but everything about our past is broken beyond repair. I want to give in to whatever this is, but my pride won't let me.

His baritone voice vibrates on my breasts. "I missed you."

I want to shoot into survival mode and resist, but the heat in my chest takes me back to that night, in my bed, when he made me feel like we would be together forever. His charm turns me on, and I envision us laying down in this position. This isn't exactly a buddy hug. His heart thumps on my collarbone, and his breath increases with each second. His forearms are hard as metal, and my hands aren't substantial enough to fit all the way around them, so I slide my hands around his neck. I almost forget that I'm hugging my best friend.

"Cash, friends don't hug like this," I say slowly, blinking with seriousness in my face.

"So does this answer your question?" he asks. I look in the mirror behind him and see our reflection with my arms around him like he's my man. I swallow hard. "I've always been in love with you, Sym." He slowly puts me down.

"Does my brother know that?" I fold my arms.

"Not yet, but now that Todd's out of the picture, maybe we can explore some things. See you at midnight," he says, slowly opening the door. "Cash, wait... That's not a good idea.

"I'm flattered, but you're my best friend. I don't want to ruin what we have, considering that it took us a while to even get to this point, do you know what I mean?"

"I love your T-shirt. SUPER BESHIE. What does it mean," he asks, avoiding my comment. "I made this shirt a long time ago. It means I can do anything without limits, and it's a reminder to love myself with confidence. But Cash, we can't sweep the past under the rug."

"You're so sexy and smart too. Can you make me a thousand of those shirts? I can give them to my fans." His generosity totally catches me off guard.

"Umm, I'll have to think about it, Cash."

"What is there to think about? I'm pretty sure there's a lot of girls out there who need a confidence reminder." I scrunch my face.

"You might be onto something," I say, poking out my bottom lip a bit. There he goes again, boosting me up like he always does.

"Plus, your boobies make it look even better. They weren't fully grown the last time I saw them," he says, laughing.

"Bye, Cash." I push him out the door.

He turns around, and our eyes meet yet again.

He says, "All jokes aside, I got you something that I should've given you a long time ago." He steps in the hall and looks left to right before leaving.

What! That's what he leaves me with? He knows I don't have patience. *Something he should've given me a long time ago?* I look over the balcony and see Aunt Donna, my mom's sister, patting her blonde afro, licking her lips in the mirror in front of the wall table on the side of the stairs. I love Aunt Donna. She has flawless, chestnut skin with an eccentric style. She calls everybody *"Honey Bunny"*, and she's the only person I know that can make jellyfish tights look good. There she goes again with that 1980's Polaroid camera.

Oh, good, Cash's parents are here from across the street. I shut my door. Wait a minute. I grab the doorknob to open it, but it's stuck. I twist harder, and then it opens. I don't know how many times I asked my dad to fix this door.

I can hear him now, *"Sure, baby girl. I gotta get my tools out of the car!"*

My door has been getting stuck for at least a month now, and he keeps saying the same thing. I look over the balcony. Dad is downstairs staring out the window in his palm-tree shirt.

What is he doing? I saw his girlfriend Sonia park outside thirty minutes ago, so who else is he looking for? He had one hand in his pocket and the other hand holding a wooden bat like a cane. If that bat is for mom's new boyfriend, then *this party's going to blow up like collard greens in a pressure cooker.*

I stroll back into my room and shut the door. The magnetic energy between Cash, and I scares me, and I think it's a little too soon to jump in somebody else's car. I pick my phone up off the dresser. *One hundred, and twenty missed calls from an unknown number?* Don't be so obvious Todd. *What a joke.* I block him from my social media accounts and put the phone back on the dresser. I admire the dress on the bed.

It's time to take on the night like the grown woman I claim to be.

IMPERFECTIONS

S **tevie Wonder's** *"Ribbon in the Sky" muffles through the closed door. How many people did she invite? It sounds like a concert downstairs. I look in the full-body mirror behind the closet door.*

My cranberry and lace dress is still laying behind me on the bed. I stand with my black, strapless bra and black, lace thong on.

I pull the Saran Wrap from around my cardboard-flat stomach, and my thumb slips on the excess cocoa butter. I unwrap it at least three times, and it's still squeezing me. I finally get it off, then toss it in the trash. I grab the orange towel from the dresser and wipe the excess lotion off my skin.

I saw a girl do this on social media once. This has become my routine for the past six months. Maybe the marks will get lighter after a few more lotion-and-Saran-wrap treatments, and maybe I'll lose an inch off my midsection during the process.

My fingers run across the leathery, brown lines on my stomach. I sigh. Just thinking about what Todd said pisses me off. *Nobody wants a girl with stretch marks.* If he only knew how many guys I turned down to be faithful to him.

It's been four years since I lost the weight that left the visible scars of my past struggles on the sides of my stomach. Over the years, I've learned to accept my imperfections. They are a part of me, and there's no doubt about it, I love me.

But the twenty-dollar question is, how am I going to fit my body in that tiny dress? The tag read six, but it looks smaller. I step into it, and I feel like a bag of chips squeezing in a straw. I pull it up, and I struggle with the zipper, but it makes it to the top underneath my armpit. The sweetheart neckline held down my midsize, balloon boobs pretty well. I examine my hips, thighs, and waistline in the mirror. Not bad for a girl who used to be friends with a hundred extra pounds.

At one point, I'd convince myself I had thick bones, but in actuality, the fast-food trips and milkshakes contributed to my unhealthy lifestyle growing up. I used to hate the idea of giving up on my chocolate milkshakes until I came across Dr. Ian Smith's dieting book.

I read something about how throwing a little salt on something sweet can eliminate cravings, and it worked! I also made the exercise classes at the gym part of my everyday routine. The other day, I tried on an old pair of jeans, and I had to grip both sides to hold them up with enough room to fit another body inside.

If I didn't know my value, I probably would've believed those awful words Todd said. But what about the girls who aren't strong enough to punch those words? Back in high school, it seemed like the more I walked around with confidence, the more spectators fell in line and respected and accepted me. I created the BESHIE T-shirt to remind myself to love me first and to lift up my own heart, because at one point, I was so tied up into how others perceived me that I forgot about what I wanted.

BESHIE stands for bold, educated, super-hot with a curvy, pink-haired lady cartoon figure holding up a heart in place of the "I" in individual, and ends with an "E", which stands for expressed. Maybe if I sell BESHIE shirts, I could help boost somebody else's confidence and help remind somebody else how beautiful they are. If someone feels ugly, maybe I can encourage that person to stand in the mirror and say, *"I love myself!"* Maybe one day I'll open a T-shirt store. *But when will I find the time?* Cash always gives me great ideas.

I put on my mascara, foundation, and cherry lipstick and take one more final look to make sure the curls in my hair fall just right. I step out onto the balcony and see the entire foyer full of people. Half of them, I didn't know. I activate the spinner ring on my finger. Anxiety dances to the music and sends my nerves everywhere. Here we go.

I squeeze my eyes shut for a second, and now they're all naked with watermelon heads. I giggle. It takes me a while to loosen up, but I'm sure I'll get there fast now that Cash is here. I make it to the last step, and Cash is standing there pouring Gold Bubbles into a champagne glass.

I hear a kid say, "Symphony looks so good," through the music. I hear my father say, "You know, she used to be fat, right?" But I'm not going to let those words ruin my evening. Cash's chocolate eyes are stuck on me.

"Is that for me?" I say, reaching for one of the glasses of champagne out of Cash's hand.

"Here you go, gorgeous," he says, devouring the other glass without breaking eye contact as if he would rather have a tall glass of me.

"Thanks, Cash."

I hear a familiar voice behind me. I scrunch my eyebrows and turn around. "Hello, Ms. Dunmore." There stands Tevah and a chocolate man with big brown eyes, black glasses, and a goatee.

He's wearing a black suit and a black dress shirt. "Professor Fenwal? Kind of—I mean, sort of good to see you, I think."

"Sym, don't," says Tevah.

Fenwal laughs. "It's okay. I brought you a gift," he says, passing over the flowery purple-and-pink gift bag.

I throw my hands back. "What is it? I'm not touching that."

Professor Fenwal must think I have no morals. I don't accept gifts from my enemies.

"Sym!" says Tevah, her voice between shock and embarrassment.

"What?" I shrug my shoulders and roll my eyes.

Clearly, he needed to see a head doctor. *He failed my ass, then crashes my party? Who does that?* I don't trust him.

Fenwal says, "It's fine, Tevah. I'd been doing a million things today. So Symphony might be wondering why I didn't get a chance to reach out about her final grade. But at any rate. I wanted to say hello and thank you for the invite."

I give him a sour face. "But you—"

Tevah interrupts, "You're going to love the steak. It's so good! Cash, can you show Professor Fenwal where the food is?"

"Tevah, just call me Berry, that's my first name," he says.

"Come on, man. Let me show you to the kitchen," Cash says, oblivious to what is going on.

"Oh, one more thing. Don't forget to take this!" Fenwal passes me the gift bag in my free hand.

"Uh... thanks."

The guys walk toward the kitchen.

"Tevah, what's up with this guy? Has he told Mom and Dad yet? What does he mean, 'he hasn't reached out to me'? You read the email like I did, right?"

"Yeah, I read it too. Sym, let's open this upstairs." Tevah wraps her arm around my arm, pulling me upstairs with our heels clunking on the stairs through the music, and the gift bag strap dangles on my arm.

"Oh yeah, I forgot to tell you, Todd's mom sent over a gourmet cupcake with twenty-three birthday candles in it," says Tevah.

"But it's not my birthday... and why would she put a bunch of candles in a single cupcake?" I ask, swimming in irritation.

"Exactly," says Tevah.

I've always loved Todd's mother, but if Todd told her to send me a birthday cupcake to piss me off, it's definitely working. But on the other hand, she's getting up in age. She probably saw all the people coming over, and assumed it was my birthday. I don't know, and right now I no longer care.

I set the bag on the bed. We stare suspiciously as if a bomb could be inside. My heart can't take the suspense. If I don't calm down, I will literally break down in tears. So I do what any respectable twenty-two-year-old would do, I put the glass to my lips and gulp down the goldish champagne like I just finished a marathon.

"What are you doing? You can't handle liquor!" Tevah shouts. The sweet burn of white grapes and apple fizzles inside my chest. "Can you blame me?" I say, trying to catch my breath through the burning sensation.

"Sym, what if you passed the class?"

Our eyes pop open, and we freeze in place at the comment. Before I can blink, pink-and-purple floral tissue floats in the air.

I shout, "why did he use so much damn tissue paper?"

We throw it everywhere. Tevah gets impatient and flips the bag upside down. Out rolls a gray-and-white stuffed elephant and a card. I turn it around. It's wearing a black cap and gold tassels.

"Wait a minute... Is this a graduation cap and gown?" I blurt out.

Tevah picks up the white envelope.

I literally can't take the suspense anymore.

Tevah unravels the piece of paper, then covers her mouth.

"What?" I ask.

"You passed the class with a B minus."

"I passed?" I whisper in shock.

My knee pushes in the bed when I snatch the card so hard that the elephant hits the floor. *I freaking passed my class!* A hundred pounds dissolved off my shoulders. Invigorated, I blow out.

"I freaking passed?" Now I can celebrate.

Tevah does a happy feet dance. "Let's light all the candles on that cupcake, to officially set your night off right! We're moving to L.A., baby! And my sister has a new fucking job!" she shouts.

I attempt to do the butterfly dance, but my dress is so tight, I lose my balance, and my knees bump the carpet.

Tevah tries to pull me up. "I told you, you shouldn't have drank it like that!"

THE MOONLIGHT

Where's Cash? *It's dark, and the tickling goosebumps cover my arms and legs. The icy breeze brushes against my skin and blows my hair over my entire face. The pinecone smell is potent, and the wet grassy aroma lingers up my nostrils. I swear I have a thousand mosquito bites or scratches on my legs. But my arms are five-hundred-pound weights, and I'm awkwardly twisted at the waist. The bass from the music vibrates my ear, and the nail file material embeds my cheek. I'm still at the party. The car sounds are close from where I am. But I have no idea where I am. I can hear people talking. Pain shoots through the side of my head. The blue-and-white specks of light pounds to the rhythm of my pupils controlled by my pulse. I'm in a daze.*

Help! I want to say, but in my catatonic state, I am far too weak to form words out loud. How did I get here?

The moonlight flickers through my lashes before I close my eyes.

"Oh my God!" yells Tevah.

Help! I say in my mind, but nothing comes out but a wince before I slip into the darkness.

LIGHTS

I *t's 12:15 A.M., and the party downstairs is still jumping. My world couldn't be better. This morning, I broke off my engagement, by noon I got the job of my dreams, and this evening, I find out I'm graduating on time. Turns out, Fenwal accidentally sent me someone else's grade.*

But right now, by far, is the best part. Right now, the soulful music of Robin Thicke plays through the pulse speaker connected to my phone. *Give you sex therapy. Give you sex therapy...*

Colorful, blue and red lights from the Pulse speaker slowly move around the dark room. His concrete muscles glisten as I rub every solid curve of his hypnotizing chest. Cash pins me against the wall between the bookshelf and dresser. He has one hand plastered on the wall and the other exploring every curve of my cranberry dress. My arms wrap around his neck, and our tongues aggressively caress slowly with the sweetness of alcohol intensifying all my senses every second. So charming and enduring and exactly what I need right now. As much as I want to take things a step further, I have to know one thing. One thing could make or break this moment. One thing could change everything. I need to know. *What's inside the Snoopy box?*

Wouldn't you want to know?

Lust shoots down between my thighs, pushing me to completely give in. But it only makes sense. He's my best friend, he doesn't judge me, and if I robbed a bank, he would never tell. He understands even the complicated side of me. Of course, the gold music box is inside. *God wants me to be with Cash?* I just know it. Tevah's going to flip.

Cash pulls me in with his powerful hands and licks my neck for blood. I moan, melting into his chest. He slides my dress up, exposing my black panties. His baritone vibrates on my chest.

"I always wanted to be your first. I hated that Todd got to be your first," he mutters.

Well, Cash was almost my first, but that didn't work out. I think I may unblock him from my social media accounts as soon as possible.

"Cash, I want to open my gift," I moan, and my hair tickles when it brushes against my collarbone.

"What?" he asks like I said something stupid.

"What's in the Snoopy box, Cash?"

"I'll show you later, Sym. I can't wait to feel how warm you are inside."

His tongue trails over the top of my breasts, gripping my dress from underneath my arms to pull it down. My dress doesn't budge. I giggle because I know he's going to need the Jaws of Life to get me out of this dress. My wavy hair falls back to my collarbone.

"How do I get this shit off?" he says, frustrated with hunger in his eyes.

What was I doing? I promised God that I would wait for sex until I got my gold music box. The box is only a few feet away. I know it's in there! It only makes sense.

Cash grips and tugs at my dress under my arm. "Is this taped to your body?"

"Cash, we need to talk."

"Sym, I've never been this ready for anything in my entire life." The moonlight shines over his face.

Wow, there's nothing like witnessing a man beg. I need you, willpower. Don't fail me now.

"Stay right here, Cash."

I pull down my dress.

I flip up the light switch next to the door. His chest moves rapidly like he just ran ten miles, and his erection is about to break through the zipper of his black slacks. He's looking at me like I stole his cup of water. I walk over to my phone and pause the music. The king tattoo sits on the line of his inner pec and flows with elaborate music notes and lines curving around his broad shoulders and hugs his forearm. The six rocks on his abs make me clear my throat. I don't know what I'm doing, but it had to be done.

"Cash, I have to know. Honestly, it's eating up

my patience by the second!" I say convincingly.

He picks up the box off the dresser.

"Open it," he says, then kisses my neck.

I rip off every piece of Snoopy paper and let it float to the floor.

I remove the white lid, look inside, and my stomach falls to my feet. Was this some kind of joke? It's empty.

"Cash, what kind of game is this? After the day I had, you have sixty seconds to get it together before I snap!" I grab my champagne glass and gulp down my second glass. Maybe I shouldn't have done that.

He laughs.

He walks up to me and slowly grips my hand looking down at me.

"Are you inebriated? You can't see what this says? I know you may still think about what happened between us five years ago, but I hope you can forgive me and leave the past in the past. When you told me you were marrying Todd, I knew I didn't want to be without you."

Where was he going with this?

He places my hand on the left side of his chest. I run my fingertips over the beautiful writing.

"What does it mean?" I ask.

"It says Symphony."

"What?" I ask.

I take a closer look. Well, damn. It does spell my name. Now I'm confused more than ever.

"So this is what you've been wanting me to

see? This is what you should have given me a long time ago?" I point to his chest.

"Yes, the box is empty because my life has been empty without you. I put your name over my heart because you will always have it. I can't lie... when you told me you gave Todd your virginity, I literally had chest pains, and my eyes watered up. You know I'm a gangster, and we don't cry right?" He grins.

I put my hand on my hip. "Are you serious, Cash?"

"Very serious. Is something wrong?"

"Cash, you have some nerve. In high school, you promised to tell Duck you wanted to be with me! But instead, you packed your bags and barely said goodbye. Why did you leave like that? Huh?"

"Sym, think about it. What choice did I have? If I would've stayed, I wouldn't be in the position I'm in today, doing what I love—music. Not everyone gets a shot to live rent free to work on their craft full time."

"Cash, I only had a few more months until I finished high school, and you left me behind. I understand when people have to do what they got to do, but you left me. All my plans after graduation included you. We made so many plans together, and my grandma died. I needed you. Why do you think I waited so long to have sex? Why do you think I even dated shallow ass Todd? I didn't know how to get over you. I didn't know how to move on. I waited and waited and waited, until finally, I gave in, and here we are, back where we were before you left. Was it because I had more weight on me than the girls you used to date back then?"

"Sym, your weight never mattered to me."

"Cash, that's why I never told you I lost weight because something in the back of my mind told me that maybe, just maybe, you would have come back if you knew I wasn't heavy anymore. I hated that thought because it's insecure, and I'm too secure to stoop so low to consider losing weight for a man. I did it for me."

"Wow, that's tough. Sym, your dad put that big-girl complex in your head back then. I thought you were fine the way you were." I shake my head. "But that doesn't change the fact that you never told my brother about us, even after you took me to prom."

"Sym, there's more to it," he says, flustered and looks away.

"What is it that you're not telling me?" I ask. *Why isn't he responding?*

He's standing there with squinty eyes and a dent between his eyebrows. "Sym, just let it go."

"There's something you're not telling me, isn't there?" I slowly move his chin to face me, and there's hesitation in his eyes.

"Tell me," I whisper. My legs wobble a little.

Wow, this champagne is pretty strong. Sort of crept up on me like a cheetah.

"Sym. I'm sorry you can't see that getting a permanent tattoo with your name carved in my skin isn't showing how much I love you. I'm sorry I loved music just a little bit more back then. But I can't redo the past."

"Cash, even if you could redo the past, you wouldn't, remember? You loved music more."

"Sym, it's your going-away party. We can talk about this some other time." He opens the door. The party music blasts in, and he's gone.

TEN POUNDS

*T**he long,** gray chair has a blanket over it, and it's bumpy like four pillows are spread underneath. The blanket moves, followed by a snore. Who is that? How can they breathe with a freaking blanket over their head?*

So I'm not sure what kind of game this is, but this is not my room. *What time is it?* I can't see the sky through the crease of the long, teal drapes hanging over the huge window frame behind whoever's in the gray chair. The beeping noise is a high-pitched killer. As if its mission is to specifically murder my concentration. I swear I have two straws up my nostrils, and the side of my skull pounds like I ran into a wall. *Why am I groggy like I drank a bottle of Nyquil?*

This must be the hangover of all hangovers. I move my head to the center, fighting the stiffness of my neck. Directly in front of me is a whiteboard with the number 23-23 on the wall, I think. I squeeze my eyes to endure the sharpness in the back of my throat. *Is there a finger in my throat?* Whatever it is has my gag reflex on full alert. I lift my arm to pull it out, but the pinch on the back of my wrist interjects. I use my thumbnail to activate the spinner ring, but my nail scrapes against the skin of my inner finger. *Where's my ring?*

I slowly lift my arms and see a purple catheter with a thin clear tube attached.

Wait... I'm in the freaking hospital? Oh, God, there's a freaking needle in my arm! My heart flips out, and the stupid beeping speeds up behind each thump. I'm pretty sure I'm on the verge of passing out, but I can't yell for help. I can see tiny spots of blue in my vision, and my head burns like vapor rub on steroids.

What happened to me? A lady rushes through the thick, brown door with green hearts on her scrubs. She has blunt-cut bangs, tan skin, a wide nose, and curvaceous hips. She shines a light in my eyes.

"It's good to see you awake, Ms. Dunmore. Your mother brought in a sweet potato pie." She points to the pie on the thin table against the wall.

"The aroma must have rejuvenated your senses because you woke ten minutes later! What an excellent combination that is—God, love, and sweet potato pie. But I need you to calm down for me, sweetie."

I hear a woman's voice yell, "Sym!"

The blanket flies by the window, and a body jumps up. *Tevah?*

More people run in through the massive door with coffee cups in hand. It's a woman in a flowy, flower dress, and the husky, tall man with a yellow-and-blue palm tree shirt. *Mom and Dad?*

My eyelids become ten-pound weights, and I slip into the darkness.

❊ ❊ ❊

I barely move despite my efforts, and now there is a plastic oxygen mask on my face. *How long was I out?* The headache of all headaches hugs tight on my brain like a blood-pressure cuff. I shiver hard like an old Chevy on its last wheel. My breathing is uncontrollably fast, and there's nothing I can do about it.

A nurse rushes in and says, "Symphony, your blood pressure is rising. Settle down dear, I don't want you to have another panic attack. The tubes were extubated yesterday, a few hours after you woke up, so you're breathing on your own now, but with the oxygen mask to help out."

There goes that beeping again.

"Your blood pressure is still rising. I'm going to give you some medicine through your IV to calm you," says the same nurse from before.

"No, we can calm her down!" says one of the voices. Tevah and Mom stand next to me. My breathing is rapid, and I'm on the verge of passing out again.

Tevah grips my hand. Her hand is sweaty. Judging from the redness in her eyes, she hasn't slept in a while.

I can hear my father in the background saying,

"Breathe, baby girl!"

But I don't know how to breathe.

Tevah says, "Breathe with me." Tevah forms her lips like a whistle and blows out slowly.

"Catch my rhythm, Sym. You can do it."

The tranquility in her voice soothes me, and Mom's warm hand on my forehead is comforting.

"Christ, please help my baby breathe. Please, Lord Jesus!" says Mom.

Tevah sucks in air, and her chest rises. She blows out; her chest goes down. I study her movement, observing every detail, including the liquid apprehension forming in her eyes. We breathe as one, simultaneously as one. Our bond as one. The beeping slows back to its normal rhythm.

A mini flashlight shines in my eyes. "You're doing great, Symphony. Wow! The love of family can do a lot," the nurse says, smiling down at me.

"Good job, Sym," says Mom.

Tevah turns around and throws her face into her hands. Her shoulders constantly jerk. Is Tevah crying? I don't think I've ever witnessed her cry before. As much as I want to break down, I'm taken over by confusion because I still don't know why I'm here. My mother stands in front of Tevah, blocking my view. She places a pacifying hand on my arm.

A man walks in with a long, white coat and masks hanging around his neck.

"Hi, Symphony. I'm Doctor Marshall. How's my favorite patient today?"

I give a quick nudge with my shoulders.

"Symphony, do you remember what happened to you?" asks the doctor.

I shake my head. I slowly remove the oxygen mask with the taped IV still in my hand. I clear my throat a little. Mom puts the cup to my mouth, and I sip water out the straw. I feel every bit of the cool water as it flows down my esophagus.

The doctor's eyes look gravely concerned.

"Uhh... your family told me you were somehow hit with an object on the right side of your head... you actually suffered a traumatic brain injury. We found the problem rather quickly and only had to shave a skinny rectangle of hair off to put in six stitches."

His delicate finger touches around the area above my right ear. The soreness is unbearable as he slightly presses the swollen flesh on the side of my head.

The doctor says, "I'm just checking the bandage over your stitches. Oh good, the nurses covered the dressing really well. It's still a little swollen, but it's going down. When you made it to the hospital, you went into cardiac arrest, and you officially flatlined for two minutes. You're a very lucky young lady."

"I died?" I strain to say just underneath a whisper.

"Yes," he says regretfully."After we managed to revive you, you went into a coma for about forty-eight hours. You don't have internal bleeding in your brain and the skull was not fractured; however, we think one or more of your cranial nerves that affect the movement of pupils, vision, and tongue may possibly be damaged, but we won't know until the swelling is completely down. After you heal, we can do some testing to see if the nerves are damaged at all. Have you had issues remembering things before?"

"Not really."

"I will give your parents a list of clinical psychologists for you. I think you may possibly be suffering from dissociative amnesia. It occurs when a person blocks out certain details associated with a stressful or traumatic occurrence. Maybe talking about that night with your family may spark a memory. I know this is a lot to take in, but I'm here if you have questions."

I whisper, "I can barely tolerate alcohol. I had too much champagne at the party. I could have done this. I feel so stupid. I'm moving to Los Angeles. I have a new job out there." Tears slide down my cheeks. The thought of actually dying is at the forefront of my mind.

"Ms. Dunmore, right now any slip or fall could be detrimental to your health, and traveling may increase the risk of further damage. We want that nerve in your brain to properly heal. I'm sure L.A will still be there when you get better, and I'm sure your employer will understand."

"How long until she recovers?" Dad asks.

"Three to four weeks," says Dr. Marshal.

I search everyone's worried faces. Is this really happening to me? I stare off into the distance.

"Do you have any questions, Ms. Dunmore?"

I slowly shake my head.

"Feel free to reach out if you need me. I will be back to check on you in a little while."

"Thank you, Doctor," says Mom.

He walks toward the door. I don't know what to feel right now.

My dad opens the door for a man with short, black hair, a bushy mustache, and a sloppy, over-sized gray suit. He's holding a notepad and pen in one hand and tissue in the other hand, wiping his reddish nose. He looks up. "These allergies are killing me."

Squeak! The door opens widerer.

A man walks in the room. He says, "Hi. Nice to see you again, Mr. and Mrs. Dunmore. Hello, Tevah. Can I talk to her?" he says, pointing at me.

"Yeah." Dad nods his bald head.

"I'm happy to see you awake, Symphony. It's been a tough few days for you. My name is Detective Mario Fields. Can I ask you a couple of questions about what happened to you?" He blows in the tissue.

"I don't know what happened to me. I can't remember," I say dejectedly.

"Sym, what did you see? Tell him," Mom interrupts.

A flash covers my vision of the fifteen-year-old me sitting in the back seat of Mom's car, silently on the verge of a panic attack. Mom stops at a red light, turns around, and says, "Symphony, what did you see, dammit!"

Fields says, "Ms. Dunmore, are you alright?"

"Uhh? I don't remember what happened to me," I say.

The detective says,"Tevah told me that you had plans to meet up with Cash Anderson in your room. Is that correct?"

"Yes, I had plans to meet him in my room to hang out, and he showed up."

The detective passes me a skeptical eye.

"Wait a doggone minute... You had a boy in your room?" Mom says in shock.

"Laney, calm down, let her finish," says Dad.

I say, "yes, Cash and I talked, Detective." I clear my throat.

"That's it? You talked? Did Cash hurt you?" Mario stops writing on his pad and looks up at me.

"Detective, if you're implying that Cash had anything to do with this, you're wrong."

This guy is crazy if he thinks I'm going to let him blame Cash for this. I remember getting in a heated argument with Cash, but I don't think having a dispute over him leaving me to go to New York is a reason for him to try to kill me.

"Ms. Dunmore, these are precautionary questions. Was Cash the last person you were with?"

"Yes, he was but... I had another drink of champagne, which I probably shouldn't have had..."

"Did Cash attack you?" Tevah blurts out.

The detective puts out his hand to stop the interruptions.

"Cash gave me a gift box with nothing in it. I was pissed, we argued about some old childhood disagreement, and he left the room."

The detective scratches his head.

"Symphony, we think someone climbed up the tree and somehow managed to get in through your bedroom window. We don't know how you ended up on the roof. But I'm going to need to talk to Mr. Anderson."

"The roof?" I ask.

"Yes. I'm sorry. I thought you folks told her already. You were found on the roof. I thought that maybe the perpetrator panicked and wanted to buy some time to get away because that part of the roof can't be seen from the street," he says.

"I leave my window open sometimes; it can get humid upstairs. But Cash would never hurt me. He's one of my best friends. Detective, I was drinking champagne. I could have done this. I have a very low tolerance for alcohol. I probably hit my head on the windowsill," I say in a weak voice.

"The last time I drank too much, I ended up asleep in someone's bathtub ."

"I'll certainly consider that, but we have to rule out any foul play before we can close out this case. Is there anyone who may want to get even with you?"

"Well, I just broke up with my fiancé , Todd. He said he wouldn't allow me to break up with him, and he showed me his gun on the video chat, threatening me. Well, it was an indirect threat."

"What!" shouts everyone in the room. "That muthafucker!" says Dad.

"We talked to your ex-fiancé, and his alibi checks out. He was with his mother when she got admitted to the hospital at least three hours before you got here, and you were missing for one hour. But I think I'll talk to him again."

I swallow. "Tevah, remember that girl in the red buggy?"

"Oh, yeah. There was some creepy-looking lady outside, watching our house in the afternoon that day. She had straight, black hair, pale skin, and stood about five-seven. When I asked her why she was staring at my house, she got scared and drove off," says Tevah.

"A red Volkswagen, huh?" He writes something down in his notepad. The detective puts his phone to his ear and points a "hold one moment" finger. He rushes out of the room. I watch him pace around through the crease of the door. The detective barges in.

"Symphony, everyone's social media accounts are now locked, and we have hours of video footage to review. I gotta go, but I will certainly perform a thorough investigation."

"Thank you, Detective Fields," says Dad before the detective left. I saw the rage in my father's eyes. Todd may not survive the night with my father on the loose.

"I can't wait to get my hands on that muthafucker. Nobody threatens my baby girl," my dad says, forgetting I probably did this to myself and beating up Todd won't help me remember.

"Tommy, put some sanitizer on your hands and take a walk," says Mom.

Dad presses his hand on the sanitizer dispenser on the wall. White foam fills his huge palm.

"Laney, don't let Symphony eat all that pie," he says before walking out.

"I don't understand him. Why does he say stuff like that, especially at a time like this? Does he really think I'm going to eat an entire pie by myself? Have I ever eaten an entire pie by myself?" I whisper.

The nurse's expression of concern catches my attention. I roll my eyes in exasperation. Tevah runs her fingers through her now pink hair, then puts her hand on her hip. Mom stares at the ground and shakes her head in embarrassment. Her bob moves then falls back in place.

"When Symphony is discharged, any form of stress can trigger a panic attack and may cause her blood pressure to go up again. We don't want her to be stressed in any way," says the nurse.

"Oh, please excuse her father. I'll have a chat with him about that. I agree, he needs to work on his delivery, but he does mean well. My husband, well, my soon-to-be ex-husband, is a little paranoid because his mother weighed over four hundred fifty pounds and died from complications with her diabetes. So he's afraid the same thing could happen to Symphony. This is all tearing him apart inside, especially being downstairs having a good ole time when Symphony was found."

I never knew the reason behind my father's torturous words. Now it all makes sense. But not exactly something I want to deal with right now. I look around the small room.

"Where's my phone?" I say.

"The police took it in as evidence. But you can use this cell phone," says Mom, handing me her old flip phone.

"Where's Duck? Did he have to go back to the base in Texas?"

Mom opens her mouth to speak, but Tevah interrupts, "Duck's on his way. He texted me. He had to meet with one of his lieutenants downtown."

I need my brother right now. He has a way of fixing things.

I remember what he did for me for junior prom. I didn't have a prom date and silently moped about it, because almost everyone got asked to go, except me.

One day, I went into the garage to put my clothes in the washer. Tools click-clacked while Duck and Cash worked under the Mustang hood. Duck looked back at me. "Hey, dude, don't you have prom in a few days?"

"I'm not going."

"Why?" asked Duck.

"I don't want to talk about it. I just don't want to go."

"What about if Cash took you?" Duck suggested.

Cash bumped the back of his head on the hood when he stood up.

"Uhh? Me?" Cash said and pointed at himself.

"I'm not some charity case, Duck," I said before I stormed back in the house. Cash followed me in the house and begged me to reconsider for an hour and topped it off with a smile. That was the first time I took a good look at him and never appreciated such a beautiful, pearly smile on a man before. I'm sure he looked at me like I was Duck's chubby little sister and had no plans to take things past prom night. But I thought, well, at least I had a date.

I found it odd that Duck came up with the idea, considering how he scared off any guy who came near me in the past.

Maybe he blamed himself in the back of his mind. But this gesture was a clear indication that my brother wanted to see me happy.

Cash picked me up in his old-school BMW and wore a sleek, black bow tie and suit, and I wore a long, blue dress that draped over my curves with a blueberry shawl over my shoulders. Thank God I listened to Mom and wore a girdle to smooth out the bumpy areas of my thick legs.

After prom, we talked for hours. I don't think my brother thought for one second that Cash would be remotely interested in me, and I'm sad to admit that my expectations were pretty low. But something magical happened. We had so much more in common than we thought. We both share a love for entertainment, *and we couldn't stop talking about politics and women empowerment. He made me feel like nothing else mattered, but me. Cash parked in front of his house across the street from my house. He ran his fingers down the side of my cheek and kissed me on the lips. That was the first time I ever felt fireworks instantly, and I literally saw a twinkle in his eyes. We both decided to keep our newfound chemistry to ourselves.*

"I hope I did this to myself. I don't want to see Duck flip out on somebody," I say, looking back and forth at Mom and Tevah standing next to each other.

Mom holds my hand. "I wish I had the right words, Symphony."

Tevah sits in the gray chair, hunching over with both hands rubbing her forehead.

Mom says, "I'm so sorry this happened. Your father found his old rocking chair from the garage and put it on the porch. He's been sitting there on the porch rocking back and forth with his pistol because he thinks somebody did this to you. Bless his heart. I don't think he's slept since you've been in the hospital. The neighbors are scared. We've barely seen anyone outside."

Mom holds my hand. "I stayed for hours watching you the other day. The doctor told us there was a possibility of you staying in a coma for days or maybe years. It tore me up inside. I made your favorite—sweet potato pie—and kept it fire hot so the scent could fill the room. I prayed over it and asked God to bring you back. I want you to know there's no way, no way, I would give up on you. No way." She wipes her face.

All I can do is listen while I try to comprehend the process of being told to live in a bubble for three weeks. So I do the only thing I can do—lay here, listen, and be thankful that I'm alive.

A TOUGH WEEK

*T*he orange rays *of the evening sun settle down on the West. It's been two weeks since the party, and I'm finally home. Dad holds out his arm and supports my weight as I climb out the passenger seat. My eyes sting from the chilly breeze. I let go of Dad's arm to take a few steps on my own, and my foot slips on a tiny dime of a rock. But I shoot out my arms to catch my balance.*

"Baby girl!" Dad rubs the back of his bald head. I'm sure his paranoia skyrocketed to heaven.

Way to go, Sym. You almost let a tiny rock take you out.

"I'm fine," I say, walking on my own up the driveway with Dad's hand a few inches away in case I slip again. Cash's mom, Sheila, is across the street. She has on a black jumpsuit, red pumps with her hair in a long straight ponytail. She opens up the mailbox at the end of the driveway and hesitantly waves with a smile.

I've known her my entire life, even danced down the soul-train line with her at the last block party. *I almost permanently died, and she smiles and waves? Why is everybody acting so weird?*

First, Tevah interrupted Mom when I asked about Duck, and now Sheila? And where's my brother? How can a person be on their way to see you for two weeks when they're in town unless he's driving from another dimension, you know what I mean?

I throw Sheila a peace sign with my fingers.

"Hey, baby girl, I installed new security cameras all around the house," Dad says, walking on the side of me while pointing at the security cameras on the side of the garage.

I walk through the garage into the kitchen, through the dining room, and straight to the empty foyer. No more balloons. It's empty like my emotions.

I observe the wooden balcony. No more banner with my name on it. I turn left into the family room, and the photos catch my attention. It's me, Mom, Dad, Duck, and Tevah. We all had on red snow coats standing in the cloud-white snow from five years ago. I can't help but see the ski trip for what it is—the last trip I would've taken with my family had I died.

I don't know what to feel right now, but the greatness of being alive supersedes my fear of not knowing what happened to me. Any grudges I ever had are now gone. It's as if God pressed the reset on my emotions and filled my heart with peace. No rage, no sorrow, but gratefulness. I'm grateful to breathe, walk, and see each member of my family. Well, except Duck. *Where is he?*

I sigh. He never showed up at the hospital. If they sent my brother back to the military camp, I'll be pissed, but it's not like him not to call. But they keep saying he's coming. Mom has this look in her eyes. The what-ifs... *like what if I never woke up?* My mom holds my hand, and Tevah puts an arm around me.

What would their lives be like without me? The amount of anguish bubbling up is unbearable as I imagine my sister checking her text messages, scrolling down a long history of messages between her and me, only to realize I would never text her back.

And my mother, being haunted in desolation, even tortured, every time she walked by a bedroom that once was mine, in a trance, deep in sorrow, staring at the spot in front of the dresser mirror where I used to twist my hair and practice my commentary analysis... viewing an empty spot I would never stand on again.

My father, I can't imagine the amount of guilt he would feel about never putting up those security cameras when Mom asked him to a long time ago... the guilt of procrastination which could have answered so many questions about the night that his baby girl died... but realizing all his questions would possibly remain unanswered because she was gone now.

And Duck, my big brother, at war with himself for not showing up to save the day as he always did to protect his baby sister, even though I'm almost positive I did this to myself.

"We got your back, sis!" Tevah says, trying to fight back tears. My father barges in the living room like he's been working all day. I didn't hear him and Mom argue at all on the way home. But I'm glad he's still here. When he sees us, he stops and takes a breath, and sadness covers his face. It's like he's trying to hold his composure.

"Laney, I checked all the locks on the windows. Believe me, ain't nobody coming in here."

"Thank you, Tommy," Mom says. As Tevah walks me upstairs, I see that Grandma Bonnie's door was shut. Who shut it this time?

❊ ❊ ❊

Year One with Grandma Bonnie

The day Grandma Bonnie moved in, she walked through the front door with Dad, and she had on her flower muumuu dress and Homer Simpson house slippers she asked him to buy her, which looked strange seeing an old woman dragging around a cartoon head with her foot in his mouth. And her feet never left the ground, so it sounded like scraping paper sliding across the wooden floor. Crazy thing is, she didn't even say hello to us. She just shuffled on past us like she was the queen of the world.

"Say hello," threatened Dad.

"Talofa," Grandma Bonnie said through her congested breathing, which meant hello I assumed.

Definitely, a rocky start, especially when we spent

hours preparing the downstairs guest room so that Grandma would be comfortable. That was the beginning of three torturous years.

Grandma Bonnie spent most of her time in bed, even though she wasn't bedridden, but I guess being waited on hand and foot was a reason to be lazy as hell. When she did get up to use the bathroom, the entire house knew it because we heard those Homer Simpson slippers scraping around the wooden floor. Grandma Bonnie barely left her room at all. She spoke in Samoan most of the time and English when she conveniently wanted something, but she never said thank you. She never said thank you when we delivered food to her room, cleaned her bathroom, or cleaned her clothes and sheets throughout the week. She would just turn her nose up like we were supposed to clean up after her. She spent most of her time on her Homer Simpson–cased phone and ordered stuff on Amazon. I'm not sure what her infatuation was with Homer Simpson, especially at eighty years old, but we would laugh behind closed doors.

Duck would whisper, "Poor Homer, forced to look under Grandma Bonnie's dress all got damn day."

I remember the morning the delivery guys, dressed in blue, came hauling in a huge, flat Amazon box with Dad. It was addressed to Grandma Bonnie. Duck, Tevah, and I thought it was a fifty-inch TV. They leaned it against the wall, and one of the delivery guys handed my father a small package, the size of my hand. My father signed for it, and the men left.

"The little package is for Symphony!" yelled

Grandma from the guest room. Dad handed me the package. I couldn't believe what I was seeing. Why would Grandma buy me diamond hoop earrings? The package read: fourteen-carat white gold.

"Spoiled," said Duck and Tevah simultaneously.

I walked into Grandma Bonnie's room. She was propped up with a bunch of pillows behind her back in the middle of the tall bed with the remote control pointed at the television on the stand, next to the door entrance. "Thank you for the earrings, Grandma," I said.

"Yeah, yeah, yeah," she said, still flipping through the channels. I remember thinking, 'Is Grandma finally coming around to understand that we are her family? Was this some type of peace treaty? Did she raise the white flag?'

"What in the world!" screamed Mom from the living room.

I headed back in the living room, and everyone looked shocked, staring down at a huge picture frame. The picture was a pale man with brown eyes, long, straight, brown hair to his shoulders, and he was dressed in a white robe with a compassionate smirk on his face. The Amazon receipt read, Jesus.

Fire shot out Mom's ears, and she shook her head repeatedly, but her hair did not fall back into place. Mom marched to the fireplace and grabbed the Bible off the mantle.

"Tommy, I will not have a picture of Cesare Borgia in my house!" She sprung the Bible open and flipped through it like a crazy person.

"The King James Bible in Daniel 7:9 mentions that the hair of his head was like the pure wool, and in Revelation 1:5, it mentions his feet being unto fine brass as if they burned in a furnace!" Mom walks up to the picture and points at it.

"So please tell me, does this man's pale complexion look like fine brass burned in a furnace? Does his straight hair texture look like wool? This is not my Jesus! And I will not have this idolatry in my house! The Bible says we ought to keep His commandments, and I plan to do just that!" she said sternly.

Our heads turned simultaneously toward Grandma's room when we heard a congested snicker from the guest room. Someone found this moment amusing—Grandma Bonnie—someone who acted like they didn't speak very much English. Just when I thought Grandma Bonnie threw in the towel, she threw in a fake Jesus to piss off my mother.

"Come on, Laney. She's an old woman, just let her have this one thing," Dad said, sounding like a mama's boy. Mom didn't speak to Dad for a week after he hammered down the huge picture frame above Grandma Bonnie's headboard. It was like Grandma strategically made Dad place it there so it would be the first thing we saw when we walked in or by the room. It took Dad two hours and three guys to make sure the picture was secure. After the fake Jesus picture, Grandma Bonnie took disrespect to a new level. She blatantly talked bad about my mother in Samoan while my mother stood in the guest bedroom folding Grandma Bonnie's clothes. We could tell because Dad pointed his finger

at Grandma Bonnie like a child. I wanted to curse Grandma out so bad for treating my mother that way. To think, I actually felt sorry for her Negative Nancy ass.

"Symphony, don't you go disrespecting the elderly. We didn't raise you that way. Your grandmother's health is deteriorating, and the last thing I want is for your father to blame me for anything that could contribute to your grandmother's health. God still wants me to take care of her, even if she is an old bitter bat," Mom said, and we laughed.

The picture of Cesare Borgia was huge, so every time we walked up and down the stairs, we saw the fake Jesus staring back at us.

One day, Mom grew so frustrated that she shut Grandma Bonnie's door. A few seconds later, I could hear those Homer Simpson slippers scraping and sliding across the floor then a creak in the door. Duck, Tevah, and I even got in on the game Grandma played. So anytime we saw the door open, we would close it, then hide on the stairs ready to close it back when Grandma opened it again. One day we closed it eight times. That's when I thought, 'Maybe, Grandma Bonnie wasn't too sick after all.'

❋ ❋ ❋

When Tevah and I make it up the stairs, I can't help but notice the yellow police tape in front of the entrance of my room. Tevah guides me to the guest room next door, which is her old room.

"Why would I want to stay in the guestroom?"

"Well, we all thought it would be best if you stay in the guestroom since the police sort of took some of your stuff," she says, skating around the words.

"What! What did they take?" I ask in irritation.

"Why did you let them take my..." I stop. I almost lost my life. *Why would I care if they touched my stuff? Not like I could have taken my stuff to heaven.*

"C'mon, Sym. It would be like old times when we used to sleep in my bed as kids. We can play card games and talk."

"You're a little too excited. Weirdo," I say, raising an eyebrow. She makes a ridiculous face, straining and shaking her head repeatedly like she's freezing. Eight seconds go by, and she's still shaking, and her now blue hair bangs are flipping back and forth. "Alright, just don't make that stupid face anymore," I whisper.

Tevah says, "deal." She straightens up with a smile as if she won.

I don't feel like myself, and it's like I'm a passenger taking a ride in someone else's body. I'm usually worried about something, but right now, I'm not. But I do miss my brother.

As soon as we walk in, the smell of sweet potato pie enters my nostrils, but this time, it's coming from the scented candle on the nightstand. How sweet. My Snoopy slippers are in front of the silver-and-white bedding. A plastic jar of Red Vines is on the nightstand, and the big, wooden dresser has get-well-soon balloons, flowers, and farewell gift bags from the party on top and on the floor.

"Wow. I've never gotten this many flowers and gifts before at one time."

"Yup. You got a lot of people who love you!" says Tevah. The sight of the bed makes my eyelids heavy. My body's worn out. I hadn't gotten much sleep from all the constant interruptions by the nurses' and doctors' shift changes. But at least my head doesn't hurt as bad, but my stomach's a little sore, and I don't know why. Tevah pulls out a Wonder Woman adult onesie from a pink bag.

"You're putting on a onesie? Tevah, really?"

She's looking at me like she has my night all planned out. She digs her hand in the bag and pulls out a Snoopy onesie too. "This one is yours."

"Oh no, it's not! Tevah, I'm not ten anymore." She bats her big blues and pokes out her bottom lip like a baby.

"Give it here, Tevah," I say reluctantly. We slip on our pajamas.

"I got the right side!" Tevah quickly yells.

"I'm the one fresh out of the hospital. Don't you think I should choose which side of the bed I want to sleep on?"

I've always slept on the left side of the bed. But I wonder how far I could get my way around here since they all think they know what's best for me. Like what my mom said to me on the way home today.

"Symphony," she had said, "why run off to L.A.

when you can live here rent free with your mother?"
And my dad. "Baby girl, don't eat too many of those
chocolate puddings when you get home. Remember
what that junk food did to you last time."

Tevah tilts her head and crosses her arms waiting for my next move. I slowly sashay to the right side of the bed and sit. I rub my hand over the top of the comforter and hit the soft fabric a few times.

"You're in luck. I'll take the left side after all," I say with a teasing grin.

"Great," she says through her teeth. I want to torture her some more, but I'm exhausted.

"Oh, wait, I got a surprise for you." I scrunch my face like she just told me a bad joke. I fold my arms. Tevah sits on the bed and uses the remote to activate the DVD player and points the remote at the flat-screen television on the wall. I look down at my short, blue nails. I wonder if they would have buried me with this same color.

"Hi. My name is Betsie Sue, and I want to bake with you! Let's get started!" says the overly excited redheaded woman on the screen. She's wearing a long, white chef's hat.

Anger builds inside of me. I want to punch something, but I don't know why. "I remember this show. Every time she put food in the oven, the crowd would chant 'bake, bake, bake!' with dramatic music behind it all." I quickly shake my head, and my eyes widen. "Turn it off! Turn it off, now!"

Tevah points the remote controller and turns it off. "What's wrong? You used to love this show when you were a kid."

I blurt out, "No, I don't like it anymore."

Her head cocks to the side.

"Umm, I'm a little tired," I add. Tevah shrugs and turns it off.

"Sure, okay. Anything you want, sis."

A PROMISE

*T**his morning**, the room is bright, and the sun shines through the window onto Tevah. I gasp. Her palm props up her head, and her eyes are plastered on me. Her hair is now pink; it was blue the night before.*

"Umm... Are you watching me sleep? Weirdo." She gives a slight grin.

"When you were in a coma, I stared at you for hours and waited for a glimpse of movement. And I got it too. Right when I started singing, 'Jesus loves the little children', your lips curled, and your eyelids tightened. I ran to the nurse's station and found out that random movement was normal in the condition you were in. I swear part of me started to leave my body. I thought if I could send you good vibes, you would open your eyes."

Water forms in her eyes. "That first day, I made a promise to God that if He woke you, I would consider not cursing anymore."

"Tevah, you gave God a 'you might stop cursing' promise?" I whisper.

"Yeah, but I'm going to really try." We snicker.

"I never thought something like this could happen to you. I mean, you're the good one. Never in trouble." She pushes back tears. "Don't think I'm soft because I'm tearing up."

"Don't worry, Tevah. You'll always be tough in my eyes." She grins.

"Sym, do you remember how Grandma died?" she asks.

"Yeah. She died in her sleep like Mom said because of her diabetes. I was there too, duh. Why wouldn't I remember that?"

"You're right. I was just checking to see how much you remember. Back at the hospital, when Mom asked what you saw, your eyes were open, but it was like you drifted off somewhere else." I sit up and lean back on the cold headboard.

"I don't know if it's an old dream, but I had a vision of us back when we were in high school. You were in the passenger seat, and Mom was driving. Mom stopped at a light, and you both looked back at me. Mom yelled, 'What did you see, dammit!' Like if I didn't tell her, she would do something bad to me."

At this point, Tevah's looking at me like snakes are crawling from under my pink bonnet on my head. "Mom said dammit? Yeah, right! And what do you mean you thought she would hurt you?" says Tevah.

"Yes, I did, but it's not real." I pull the blanket over my shoulders. Tevah breaks out into laughter.

"Mom? I mean, yeah, she has a tough side, but she doesn't even yell. She just throws stuff when she's mad. You know how she is."

"I know. I thought it was sort of weird too," I say. "Hey, Tevah, do you remember when you stole the postal truck?"

"Yeah. He shouldn't have gone inside Ms. Wallace's house to hump on her old, married ass."

"Sym, do you think he went down on her?" I stick my tongue out in disgust.

"Dang it, Tevah! I want to eat at some point today. Yuck, I don't want that visual in my head." We hurl out twenty feet of laughter.

"I'm glad you're home, Sym. You're the closest person to me. This entire thing puts things in perspective too. Like when I punched the blonde in Todd's apartment, what if she died when she hit her head on the floor? Then we both could have gone to jail, you know?" Tevah says.

"Well, that girl deserved everything she got that day," I say with a serious expression.

"Sym, I want to try being a little softer and shit. You know, try something new."

"Well, that's good, and you just cursed."

"My bad, God." She turns around and grabs something from the nightstand.

"I almost forgot to give you your anxiety ring back."

She places it on my palm. Tevah's the only person that knows what the ring is for.

"You know what? I don't think I need this anymore."

"Well, I still want you to take it easy, Sym."

"I don't know. I might end up in the hospital again if you keep blowing your hot breath in my face." I fan away the funk with my hand.

"Bitc—" she mutters. Mom walks in with a silver platter of eggs, pancakes, turkey bacon, and her famous Memphis oven-fried potatoes. The smell instantly makes me happy. "Mom, are you alright?" Tevah asks.

Mom is smiling from temple to temple. "I'm fine. You two laying in the bed reminds me of when you were kids."

"One kid is still missing in action," I say, looking around.

"Don't worry about that. Duck should be on his way soon. I am sure of it," Mom says.

They have been saying that for the last two days. Something's going on, and I'm going to get to the bottom of it.

"Mom, thanks for the royal treatment," Tevah says.

"Yeah, thank you!" I join in. "You're welcome. I'll be back later to check on y'all." The door shuts behind her.

"Tevah, can I use your phone?" She reaches over and picks up her phone from the nightstand. "Who are you calling?"

"Duck, but the phone is ringing and ringing." I start dialing another number.

"Who are you calling now?" I put my finger in

front of my mouth.

"Shush, I'm calling Cash."

"He's probably busy..." she anxiously says.

"Hello, this is Cash."

"Cash? Umm, hi. You okay?" Tevah sits up.

"Sym?" His voice is higher like he's just realizing it was me.

"I'm back home. I don't know if your mom told you, but I saw her yesterday in the driveway."

He breathes out. "I'm sorry I couldn't save you," he says in regret.

"Save me? Save me from what?"

He didn't sound like the confident, opinionated Cash I knew.

"Hang up!" says a woman's stern voice in the background.

"I got to go," he says, and the line clicks.

"Tevah, what's going on? My best friend hung up on me!" She had a dumbfounded look on her face.

"Cash totally blew me off. And his mom waved at me in the driveway like I was a stranger."

Tevah shrugs her shoulders, oblivious to everything. Tevah is hiding something. I can tell by the way she scratches her arm, then sticks some eggs in her mouth from the plate on her lap.

"Tevah, cut the crap. What's going on?"

"Sym, one of the party guests may have heard me tell the detective that Cash was the last person with you when the detectives interviewed us at the hospital. They posted it on social media, so people think Cash had something to do with it. They were talking about it online before everyone got locked out of social media."

"How many people?" I ask.

"Like our entire family and a few random people commented too," she says reluctantly.

"I officially need a chocolate milkshake. He says he was sorry he couldn't save me. I don't know what he's talking about. Save me from what? My drunk self?" I sigh.

"How about I get you some strawberries or nice Habanero almonds?" Tevah says, trying to lighten the mood.

I give her an "I hate you" look and I pick up the cell phone from the bed. I gasp. "Wait a minute? What day is it? Oh my God! It's March first?" I observe the phone screen.

"Yeah, why?" she asks.

I push over the breakfast tray and head to the hallway. The fuzz of the tan carpet tickles my feet. I open the hall cabinet and scoot over the books and old shoes.

"Sym, what are you doing?" Tevah stands there with a puzzled expression.

"Just put on your clothes," I say frantically.

"Sym, you're supposed to be on bed rest. What if you fall?" she says, pulling up her black tights. I throw on my SUPER BESHIE tee shirt and blue skinny jeans.

"Where's my coat?"

She says, "Oh, it's in your room." I throw

on Dad's huge, black jacket from the guest room closet and stuff my hair in the construction hat I saw on the shelf. I see Mom's old, rusty, white flower basket. I can use this. I grab as many flowers as I can from the dresser. We walk out into the hallway, and I quietly shut the guest room door.

"Tevah, you better tell me why everybody's acting weird," I whisper, looking over the balcony to see if the coast is clear.

She sighs. "Alright, I'll tell you in the car, but I'm driving. The last thing we need is to crash before Mom throws the house at us for sneaking out."

Why am I letting Tevah drive my car again? Lord, help us.

TEVAH'S SIDE OF
THE STORY

"*T*evah, did you* leave a note for Mom?"
asks Symphony.

"Yeah, I left it on the bed."

"Well, I'm waiting." Symphony folds her arms.

"Sym, what are you waiting for?"

Maybe if I play dumb, Sym will get annoyed and give up, but judging by the desperate look in her eyes, she isn't going to let this go. I don't blame her.

I drive down the concrete slope road of Mount Forty. I glance over at Symphony again, and she has a serious dent above her freckled nose. She's in no mood for games.

I can't talk my way out of this shit. Oops, my bad, Lord.

"Alright... I'll tell you!"

❅ ❅ ❅

The night of the party, Tevah and Professor Fenwal had a make-out session in the bathroom. Yeah, he may have baby-kangaroo hands, but he was built like a *dinosaur down under, she thought. Tevah knew Symphony was meeting Cash at midnight, but after she and Fenwal left the bathroom, Cash had been downstairs for a while. It was one A.M., and everyone thought Symphony might have been in the bathroom upstairs.*

When Tevah checked the bathrooms, they were empty. So she went into Symphony's bedroom and saw Symphony's cell phone on the floor next to the dresser. Ms. Wallace's security garage light lit up and shone through the window. Something told Tevah to open the window to see if she could hear or see Symphony hanging out in the front yard. As soon as she opened the window, Tevah thought she heard a moan. Ms. Wallace's security light shone again, but this time, Tevah saw the leaves all over Symphony's red dress, face, and hair. Symphony's torso was on its side, and her legs crossed with her bare toes pointed to the sky. Tevah called out Symphony's name, but she didn't get a response. Tevah thought Symphony may have been drunk, but she didn't budge, and when Tevah swept Symphony's hair from over her face, the liquid on Tevah's fingers wasn't from the sprinkles of rain; it was blood. Tevah lost it. She went crazy and ran downstairs screaming.

"Dad! Symphony's on the roof! She's hurt!"

Thomas, Cash, and Duck flew up the stairs. Duck jumped on the roof, and Thomas and Cash carefully pulled Symphony in. Thomas checked Symphony's pulse and started to perform CPR. When the police and paramedics came, they put Symphony on a stretcher and rushed her to the hospital. They were all zombies sitting in the waiting room in a daze. Professor Fenwal rubbed Tevah's back as they all sat there silently waiting for the verdict. The doctor called Elaine and Thomas to talk to them privately around the corner. Duck paced back and forth in the hallway, and Cash sat on the other side of Tevah, furious like he wanted to choke the life out of whoever did what they did to Symphony. Everyone took a turn to talk to the detectives and the police in the hallways. And Todd was there too, on his cell phone, talking in Spanish. Tevah wondered why he showed up, but decided to keep quiet until she knew Symphony was fine. But when Elaine and dad came back to the waiting room, she never saw them so distraught, so defeated before. Elaine stood directly in front of Todd's feet.

"Were you the one who attacked my daughter?" *Elaine asked. Todd's eyes popped open like an egg.*

"Impossible. No, Mr. and Mrs. Dunmore, I wasn't at the party. Tevah shut the door in my face." Todd rubbed his hands through his short black hair. "My mom was admitted down the hall for asthma way before I knew Symphony was here. I had absolutely nothing to do with this... I love her."

"Symphony told me what happened at your apartment, and I don't appreciate you treating my daughter like some rotten whore! Did you do this because she hurt your arrogant feelings?" Duck entered the waiting room and saw what was happening. Everyone was in a silent panic, terror building with each word.

"I'm going to ask you this question, and please be

truthful. Did you kill my daughter?" Elaine's tone is both accusatory and full of disgust. Everyone gasped. Tevah's heart sunk into the linoleum floor. Duck twisted his mouth.

"You did what? You killed my sister?" Duck charged at Todd. Thomas scooped Elaine out of the way when Duck swung and landed a punch on Todd's face. Todd stood, and charged at Duck like an animal. They fell to the hard floor. Cash tried to peel Duck off Todd, but Duck shot Cash a death stare and shoved him with force.

"Man, what the fuck?" Cash yelled.

"Fuck you too, bro!" Duck hollered. Cash stood there with a confused expression as Tevah cried her eyes out. Duck landed another punch to Todd's chin, and blood flew out of Todd's mouth. The cops and hospital security broke them apart.

"I absolutely had nothing to do with this!" Todd shouted and blood leaked from his mouth.

Duck turned into a wild bear, and officers couldn't hold him down or calm him. Duck broke through the officers, picked up Todd by his collared shirt, and threw him against the hard, cemented wall. Todd's slim build never had a chance.

I parked on the side of the road.

"I had no clue Todd came to the party," Sym says in shock.

"Yeah, he did."

"Tevah, where's Duck now?"

"He's in jail."

"What?" I pull back out to the street and drive.

"We all decided not to tell you because we didn't want to stress you out. The cops took him and charged him with resisting arrest, assault, and battery... you name it. The cops saw the entire thing go down."

"Duck's in jail for defending me? Why would Duck push Cash? This doesn't make sense!"

"Sorry, Sym. I wanted to tell you, but Mom and Dad didn't want to stress you out. Remember what the nurse said, no stress." I say, forcing myself to sound as cheerful as possible. I drive in the parking lot.

"Umm... Sym, I'll wait here until you're done. Be quick before Mom notices we're gone."

BAKE-BAKE-BAKE

*T**he air is** garden fresh, and the green landscape has beautifully shaped oak trees lined up everywhere that resembles broccoli. There's something angelic about this place, even with sadness in the midst from the freshly-dug graves. I pick up a white rose from the flower basket dangling my arm and place it in front of the stone on the grass.*

I look back and see the row of flowers I put down next to each gravestone, and I make sure to put an extra flower next to Grandma Bonnie. Coming here started out as a business arrangement but turned into sort of a thinking place for me. I know, kind of weird, but it's true. In the distance, I see a guy walking with a lady, and she has on a long, flowy white dress.

I squint, and it looks like Tevah's still on the phone with Professor Fenwal. I can tell because she likes to wave her arms around when she talks. I can't help but wonder why this is all happening. My brother's in jail, my best friend won't talk to me, and I can't remember how I ended up on the freaking roof. My heart is heavy now, and I want this miserable emotion to go away. Not to mention, I can't help but feel like the bake-bake-bake video has a connection to how I feel right now. Something about the video left a speck of uneasiness in my gut, and I would give anything to make it go away.

A vision covers my mind of the six-year-old me attempting to draw the back of my mother as she mixed the spaghetti noodles with the thick tomato sauce on the stove.

"Look, Mom, I drew a picture of you!" I used to love drawing stick figures of Mom and made sure to put nice hair, a dress, and tall heels for her. Back then, I wore flare dresses and bright-colored leggings to fit my little ham-hock legs. Mom loved to braid my hair in thin, single braids with colorful beads. I used to swing my hair, not because it was long, but because I loved the sound of the beads clacking together.

"All you gotta do is play along, and I'll let you pick any flavor milkshake you want," my father whispered.

My father and I both hated going to Wednesday-night Bible study because it was so boring. Tevah always wanted to go with Mom because she was in the choir, and Duck wanted to get close to some new girl who joined the youth group. So my father orchestrated a plan so he and I didn't have to go. That day, Dad and I were sitting at the kitchen island all dressed to go to Bible study when we put our plan in motion.

"Aww, man. I just remembered... I gotta stay here and work on some paperwork. Baby girl, you want to

stay with your pops?" He said it loud enough so my mother could hear. My father's company was passed down from generation to generation, which consisted of building homes in the city, so there was always something he had to do.

"Sure, Daddy," I said, in my tiny voice playing along, as Mom looked back and forth at us with a frown on her face. Mom could see right through our deceiving eyes like a fishnet.

"It's alright," Mom said. "But y'all won't be missing church on Sunday. That's for sure," she said in a threatening tone.

Dad and I peeked out the living room window and busted out in laughter as Mom backed out the driveway. When she was gone, we hopped in his white construction truck. Every time we drove to the city, Dad got me a chocolate milkshake. After we left Gunther's Ice Cream, Dad drove around the corner and parked his truck in front of a blue apartment building.

"Daddy, who lives here?" "A friend of mine."

My eyebrows sunk. "Don't worry. We won't stay too long. I gotta get some paperwork." I found it unusual for my father to choose to go there when it was supposed to be our time to hang out, especially when the paperwork thing was made up. "Dad, did your company build these apartments?"

"Yeah, baby girl." Dad knocked on apartment 330 on the first floor. A lady opened the door. She had straight, brunette hair with a long strip of pink in her bangs. She wore a short pink robe with a thin pink belt tight around her waist, but the line between her

massive breasts was exposed a little more than what was appropriate. My mother always said it's okay for a lady to show a little skin but not too much. This lady was showing way more than a little.

"Hey, there. What's your name?" she asked. Her voice sounded a little raspy.

"Symphony."

"My, my, my… that's a pretty name."

"Thank you," I said, looking around. The living room was small and smelled like apples and cigarettes. The aroma burned the inside of my nose.

"Baby girl, you go ahead and sit on the couch, and don't you go snooping around," said Dad. I nodded and sat on the edge of the purple loveseat.

The lady with the pink hair flipped on the television across from me and then pressed play. I couldn't figure out why she turned the volume up so high. The mini black speakers shook and vibrated sitting on the stand next to the television.

"Hi! My name is Betsie Sue, and I want to bake with you! Let's get started! Today, we're making pizza!" Back then, I used to love that show. It came on every day after school.

I used to yell, "Bake-bake-bake!" right along with the audience when she put something in the oven. Dad and the lady left the room, and then I heard a door shut. But I can't correlate how the baking show could cause this terrifying feeling in my stomach.

✽ ✽ ✽

I pick up the clear glass box I had on the side of the

flower basket. Inside is a 2003 mini Corvette Convertible displayed in the center. I kneel down, and I place it on the side of the headstone.

"I didn't have to put flowers on these stones when I worked here," says a guy with a deep southern accent. I gasp and jump back. The basket bounces on the grass, tips over, and the flowers spill out. Standing in front of me is a guy with dark, reddish-brown hair with both hands in the pockets of his sweat jacket. He looks like he's in his late twenties. His thick eyebrows were adorable, and his textured-fohawk haircut a bit edgy with a short, scruffy beard. He has broad shoulders like he hits the gym, and his dimples are making me shy... like right now.

"It's just something that I do by choice," I say, picking up the flowers.

"Let me get that." He bends down to help, and his black shades fall off. The wind blows my hood back, and my hair unravels out of my twisted bun. I use my hand to fix my disheveled coils, and it falls on both sides of my face.

His green eyes blast open. "Lawd have mercy and bless me on a Sunday. You're a girl!"

"Of course I'm a girl, and you're a boy," I say, snatching the basket out of his hands. "But do you always dress like this?"

I look down at my dad's large construction jacket, which sort of looks like a jacket dress. *What am I supposed to say?* My room is taped off because a potential crime took place, and my stuff is trapped in the room? I say, "I was in a rush. So what?"

"Besides, the gold is peeling on your Muhammed Ali shirt. Did you wear that on purpose?" I cross my arms.

"I beg your pardon. This is my lucky shirt. My daddy passed this on to me," he playfully says."Humph. So tell me, it looks like you put a flower on at least twenty graves. What if you gave a flower to a guy who used to torture cats?"

"Well, if he tortured cats, I'm pretty sure he regrets it now." I raise an eyebrow.

"Humph." He snickers.

"I feel what you're stepping in."

"Huh?"

"I feel what you're stepping in. It means I get it... I know what you mean."

"You're not from around here, are you, cowboy?"

"Nope. I used to live here for a few years back in high school, but after I graduated, I moved back to Texas, so I'm just here for a couple of days. Was it the accent? I guess it's a dead giveaway." He laughs.

His rough finger accidentally brushes against my hand when he puts some flowers back in the basket. He takes a long sniff.

"Damn, your hair smells good. Lavender?"

"Yes. Most men wouldn't have guessed that." The wind blows my hair back, knocking off my hat again, so I use my finger and put my hair behind my ear. "It wasn't this windy when I got here," I say, throwing the stupid hat in the basket.

He twirls the toothpick to the other corner of his mouth. "Can I ask you something?"

"I don't know." I throw him a skeptical side-eye. He reaches over near my elbow and strokes my hair.

"Soft. Is this your real hair?"

"What kind of question is that? It's on my head, isn't it? And why are you touching my hair? Do I look like a freaking pony? For all I know, you probably had that hand up some horse's ass before you came here," I say, giving him a death stare.

He balls his huge fist in front of his face and coughs. I think I threw him off his game a bit.

"Maybe I'm not conveying my words correctly. I didn't mean to offend you. Truth is, I think everything about you is beautiful." He sucks his teeth.

"Are you flirting with me right now? Here?" I say, pointing down at the grass.

"I can't help myself." He scratches his head and gives me puppy-dog eyes.

Yeah, I said it. He's giving me freaking puppy-dog eyes in a cemetery!

"I got another question though," he says.

"Oh, I'm not surprised." He squints as if he is conjuring up something good to ask.

"Out of all the flowers you put on all these here graves, what made you put a little car on this one?" he says, pointing to the tombstone behind me. I look back at the tombstone like I've never seen it in my life. The name on the tombstone is Popsicle. No basic first and last name, just Popsicle.

"I don't know. I didn't mean any harm or disrespect. Did you know Popsicle?" I ask, embarrassed.

"I used to intern here, so I used to see the families some times," he says.

I put my hair behind my ear. "Well, in that case, can you answer a question for me?"

"Oh, so now you got a question?" He smirks.

"How did he die? Do you know?" I mutter.

"How do you know Popsicle is a he?"

"I don't know. I just assumed." The phone buzzes, and he puts his hand in his back pocket to stop the ringing.

"Listen, umm... I gotta go."

"It's fine. How about we meet up later, and I'll tell you about Popsicle?"

I hesitate. "Uhh... I don't think that's a good idea."

"I'll be at my friend's boxing gym at the old Sugar Mill later. I'm only in town for a couple days. I promise I'm not crazy."

"I appreciate the gesture, but I don't go out on dates after five minutes of meeting someone."

"It's not a date. It's more like a snack. And it's been at least nine whole minutes."

"A snack?" I ask.

"Yeah. We'll just talk. There's a vending machine full of chips, donuts, and M&Ms. I'll let you pick whichever one you want. There's always a lot of people there too. You don't have to worry about anything."

I tilt my head. "Sorry, I can't."

"What do you mean?" He pouts like there's no way a woman could ever reject him.

"Oh, I see. Is this the first time a girl told you no?"

"Yeah, I had a girl tell me no. I remember it like it was yesterday. I cooked a big, juicy steak on the iron pan and threw in some onions until they turned nice and brown. I finished the master-piece off with some steamed asparagus and pota-toes on the side. I cut into it, and the brown juice flowed onto the plate. Humph, I stuck a piece in my mouth, and it tasted so good I offered a piece to my dog, Lucy, and she turned her nose up at it. Ain't that something? So yeah, I had a girl turn me down before," he says with a serious expression.

"Smart ass," I say, watching his humorous eyes get a kick out of my annoyance.

"You asked, darling," he says with a snicker.

"Hey, get away from her!" a voice yells from a distance. We both jolt back at the sound of a woman's voice from afar. I gasp, taking a quick, deep breath. The woman has pink hair, blue jeans, and a purple jacket.

My eyes widened. "That's my sister—I mean sister-cousin. I got to go!"

"Wait! What's your name? I'm Bryson." A red

rose fell from the basket on my arm.

"My name is Rose, and by the way, I grew this hair from my own scalp!" I say sarcastically before rushing off. I grab Tevah by the arm. "Calm down. We were just talking," I say, pulling her to the parking lot.

AFTER WISHES

I **shut the** *passenger door. What guy drives around with a "Shake Something" sticker on the butt of his car? The mini blue Toyota had a faded roof and dents on the outside passenger door with silver scrapes like it had been sideswiped at least ten times. I'm all for not having a new-car payment, but driving around with a "Shake Something" sticker for the world to see didn't really fit him at all. But one thing I don't trust, especially now, is a stranger. Okay, I lied about the cars. But what would I say? Yeah… umm… some random guy came over to my house and asked me to put a toy car on Popsicle's grave. Does that sound believable? I think not.*

Back then, I had just turned eighteen. I remembered organizing my bookshelf when I heard a deep voice downstairs talking to Mom. I walked downstairs to find a middle-aged man sitting on the sofa in a business suit. He had spiked, blond hair and a ridiculously long beard that twirled down into a single curl. Mom poured coffee into his cup on the table between the couches. He had a black suitcase tucked under his arm like he had a rare, ancient diamond from Africa.

"What's the name of the place you work for

again?" Mom asked.

He spoke in a drawn-out, monotonous tone. "The After Wishes Foundation, ma'am. We are a high-end service that fulfills the last wishes of individuals who have perished. My client has requested for your daughter to place a small item on a tombstone on the first of March each year for five years," he said, sounding like a college professor.

"No, my daughter's not interested, Mr. Lucas, but I need to be getting ready for Bible study," Mom said.

"Mom, why would you say no? What if Tevah wants to do it?" I blurted out.

They both look in my direction. Mom didn't even ask Tevah if she wanted to do it or not. I mean... this weird dude wasn't asking for too much.

"Symphony, he's here for you," she said.

"Me? Are you sure you came to the right place?" I pointed to the wooden floor.

"No, sir. My daughter is not interested. You ought to be going, sir," Mom said.

"I'll do it!" I blurted out.

"Symphony, you're not old enough to make these types of decisions. Excuse me, Mr. Lucas." She grabbed my arm and walked me into the kitchen.

"Mom, I'm eighteen now. I'm not a kid anymore," I whispered.

"Symphony, what if his client works for the Italian mob or something? We don't know these people," she said, looking behind her.

"Mom, I want to talk to him. C'mon, Mom. Please?" Mom sighed. We walked back to the living

room. "How did he die?" I asked.

"I'm sorry, Symphony. I am not at liberty to disclose the age, gender, or how the member died. Our clients pay fifty thousand a month for our service, so we are paid very well to keep client information confidential. We can add up to fifteen members, in which anyone of the fifteen can use our services as long as additional fees are paid. But what I can say is that you have been specifically chosen to perform this task."

"Fifty thousand dollars a month to be a member? None of my people have that kind of money, sir!" said Mom.

"How would I know what grave to look for?" I asked. "Everything you need to know is in the suitcase. If you agree, this is yours." He put the black briefcase onto his lap. It had two silver locks on the top.

"Is there some contract or paperwork I need to sign?" I said, sitting down across from him while Mom stood with her hand on her hip.

"Nope. A verbal agreement is good enough."

"I'll do it," I said hesitantly. Although I was skeptical, the words shot out, and I didn't want my mother to think I couldn't make my own decisions.

"Magnificent!" Mr. Lucas said, hopping up.

"Great doing business with you, Ms. Dunmore. Again, one item per year on the first of March," he excitedly said.

"When you have no items left, the request is fulfilled," he says, walking to the door.

Mom closed the front door and squinted her eyes at me. She wanted to know what was in the suitcase, and I wanted to know too. I stood and gently laid the suitcase on the glass coffee table. Mom was standing on the other side leaning over. I unlatched the two metal locks. The furry red interior tickled my fingers.

The piece of paper on the top read: Thank you for your participation. Please deliver only one of these items on the first of March each year. The cemetery location is found on the back. The tombstone name of the deceased has been changed to protect their identity. Client name: Popsicle. I picked up the paper, and what was underneath made my chest sink in.

"Five miniature toy cars?" Mom muttered.

It must have been a boy. They're all sports cars about two inches long with thin stickers that read the make and model. Two black, old-school cars that look like Lamborghinis, a red Bugatti, and two silver Corvettes displayed inside a clear glass box with black velvet foam holding the car in place in the center.

"Oh my God, poor baby," I said.

"I wonder how he died. This is so sad," Mom muttered.

"Remember what he said. Sometimes relatives request the service for friends and family, so it may not be a little boy," Mom said.

"The crazy thing is we don't know any rich people!" shouted Mom.

So year after year, I placed a single car on top of the horizontal tombstone with the name Popsicle. On the third year, I noticed the sign from the Sacramento Cemetery District. They had a flower and gift policy to remove items every Wednesday.

One year, I delivered the car on a Saturday—the same night I couldn't find my gold necklace. So I drove back to the cemetery to see if it fell off by Popsicle's grave, and I noticed the car was gone, which meant someone either stole the race car or the maintenance threw it away before the scheduled cleanup day. I thought maybe a raccoon could have run off with the car. But could a raccoon pick up a heavy, glass box?

I never saw anyone remotely near Popsicle's grave, so that always remained a mystery. The story of Popsicle taunted me since the very moment I put the first car down five years ago.

I started imagining Popsicle to be a little boy who could have gotten hit by a car or maybe Popsicle was a ninety-year-old woman who died from cancer but loved cars. I analyzed the scenario from every angle but came up with nothing. *Should I have accepted Bryson's snack offer?* Of course. I wanted to know who Popsicle was. I have a billion questions and no answers. Did he understand why they chose me? I had absolutely no idea. *Could he be part of the Mob?* Maybe Mom was right. I put down all five cars, so perhaps they wanted to whack me now. The ringing from Tevah's phone caught my attention as we drove back to the house. "Hello?" she says, making a right turn.

I hear a deep voice from her headset, and then she clicks the Bluetooth and hangs up on him. He calls right back. This time I look. *Unknown?* She presses the red button and sends the call to voicemail.

"Who's that?"

"Nobody important."

Here we go again.

INVITED

*W*hen we get *home from the cemetery, I heat a bag of caramel popcorn while Tevah turns on The Real Housewives of Atlanta reality show. As soon as I sit on the couch, the siren comes downstairs.*

"Where have y'all been?" Mom's stilettos clunk on the wooden floor, and her steps get louder and louder. She has on a thick, green scarf around her throat and a long, mustard-colored dress.

"Mom, it's not cold in here. You don't need a scarf. I promise you won't get sick," Tevah says in annoyance.

"I was about to go out looking for y'all!" She scowls at us like we were counting money from a robbery.

"Mom, it's spring and sixty-five degrees outside. You don't need a scarf!" says Tevah.

"That's beside the point. Where did y'all go? I've been worried sick! Tevah, how could you? Sym, why would you?" she says beseechingly.

Whenever she started sentences and didn't

finish them meant she was pissed off. But she managed to stay so poised and collected, like a school teacher disciplining her students.

"Symphony, did you not hear what the doctor said? If you slip and fall, you can end up back in the hospital or dead!"

"Mom, I'm fine," I say, sitting on the loveseat. I barely have pain at all, and the bruising is almost gone.

"Sym made me go. What was I supposed to do?" says Tevah. I throw a couch pillow at her for ratting me out.

"I don't know what I'm going to do with you girls." The front door shuts.

"You girls alright? Your mother said you went missing." Dad comes barging in.

"Hey, Dad. We're good," I say. He plants a kiss on my cheek, then walks across to Tevah and kisses hers too. Mom looks at Dad like he has nails under his construction boots after she buffed her floor.

"Tommy, I told you not to use that key. You don't live here anymore!" Mom says, frustrated.

"Laney, this is still my house and my family! I don't want to hear it! And Symphony, don't eat all that caramel popcorn!"

"But you don't even live here..." I say sarcastically. Dad throws me a smug expression and marches toward the kitchen. Mom goes right after him, bickering.

"They love each other," says Tevah, texting on

her phone.

"It's obvious," I say, flipping through the magazine.

"Daddy, my car is still making that clicking noise!" I yell toward the kitchen.

"It's alright. I'll fix it. I got to get my tools out of the car!" he yells back.

"So are you going to tell me?" says Tevah.

"What?"

"Who's that sexy guy I almost had to beat up today?" I shake my head.

"His name is Bryson."

"Did you see the Muhammad Ali bobblehead on the dash?"

"Yup!" I say. We giggle. I flip the page of the magazine.

"He actually invited me for a snack."

"A *snack*? What the hell is that?!"

"He wants to hang out. It's not like a date. He knew Popsicle's family and said if I showed up, he'll tell me about Popsicle."

"You haven't been home twenty-four hours, and you have a date?"

"Heck, no. I told him I'm not going."

"Shoot, I want to know what happened to Popsicle too. But a date with a stranger right now doesn't sound like a good idea. Maybe you should wait until things calm down around here," says Tevah.

"He's from Texas, and he's going back in a few days."

"That's cool, but I still don't think you should go."

"Gee, everyone's tossing their freaking opinions like a salad around here, and we both know I don't like salad," I say with wide eyes. She sucks her teeth and continues typing on her phone.

I flip through the magazine. It shows a picture of Steve Jobs... Steve... Steve... *Don't I know somebody named Steve?*

"Hey, Tevah do you remember somebody named Steve? I feel like I should know him." I flip through the pages.

"Yeah, I know a Steve. He was at the party."

"So, who is Steve?" I blurt out. Tevah looks toward the kitchen.

"Shush! Don't say that name too loud. I can't wait to tell you what happened."

✶ ✶ ✶

The night of *Symphony's going-away party, some family members sat at the dinner table and some stood around chatting and eating while the music played in the background.*

Symphony stood and used her fork like a microphone. "So Duck, please tell me. How do you feel about having a sister who's famous for standing up for women's rights in entertainment? Does it make you want to cry?"

Symphony reached across the table and pointed the fork in front of Duck's mouth.

"I would say I'm extremely proud, but I hate to spill

the beans. The Symphony that you all love so much is really an alien and not a woman at all!" He bowed down.

"Thank you, any more questions?" They all laughed, and Symphony shot him a smug expression.

"Don't ever touch my licorice again!" she said and sat down.

"Tevah, Symphony, sit up straight," their mother said, and then she turned to talk to one of her church friends at the table.

Thomas went back to the kitchen to stack his plate with more food. Everyone chatted, and Duck and Cash caught Tevah's attention.

Duck looked serious and felt this was vital information that Cash should know. "Cash, bro, face mites live all around your body but mostly on your face. Once the female chooses a pore, she moves in it like a house. So the male searches around for a chick, right? When he finds her, they fuck on the opening of the pore, and then boom! She's pregnant, and then she goes back in the pore to lay eggs. But the cold part is, the dude searches for another chick to bust a nut in her too! I saw this shit on social media. I swear!"

Cash chuckled. "That's tough, man," he said, showing off his perfectly straight teeth.

Tevah cleared her throat. "So this is the kind of shit guys talk about? Seriously?" she said, trying to talk through the loud music.

Aunt Donna walked in with her old Polaroid camera that dangled from the strap around her neck, and Cash got up to head to the kitchen.

Aunt Donna's blonde afro wig wiggles a little when she turns down the music on the speaker. "Hey, Laney, some pale buff man is here to see you. He says his name is Steve."

A guy walked up from behind Aunt Donna with the tightest blue jeans Tevah ever saw on a man, and she wondered if he had balls.

"Hello, everybody! I'm Steve," he said with a Kool-Aid smile.

"Hi, Steve," everyone said in unison.

Mom stood up. "Hey, honey. We were just finishing up. You want me to make your plate?"

The room gasped. Elaine wrapped her arms around Steve so tight like he came back from war. A jigsaw couldn't cut the speculation in the room. Elaine kissed him on the cheek, and the room went silent and filled with wildly-blinking eyes. Duck nervously shook his head and wondered if Mom found Tevah's weed and smoked it. Sym didn't take a breath for five seconds because she knew her father had some guns in the house. Tevah wondered if her mom would make her clean up after her dad mopped the party with Steve's head.

Cash walked back in the dining room and saw Mrs. Dunmore an inch away from Steve's face blatantly flirting like a schoolgirl. Cash did his best to pretend like he didn't notice. He put down his plate of pie, grabbed the fork, and made love to the pie like no one else was there. He'd been around the Dunmore family long enough to know that Mr. Thomas would try to kill any man who stepped to Mrs. Dunmore. And it didn't matter that Mr. Dunmore's new girlfriend, Sonia, was sitting next to him. Cash guessed her age to be at least twenty, and he felt bad for her because she kept playing with her nails, completely clueless to what was happening. Cash pretended like he didn't understand when Mr. Dunmore's girlfriend asked why everybody stopped talking. Cash was more concerned if this drama would mess up his meeting with Symphony later. Thomas coasted out from the kitchen holding a weapon.

"Hopefully, Symphony didn't eat the entire pig while I was gone," he said.

"Dad, don't do that. You know good and damn well she's not going to eat a whole pig!" Duck said sternly.

"What? I'm kidding. Baby girl, you know I'm kidding," Thomas replied, looking at Symphony.

Symphony said, "Nope, not funny, Dad." Not only did Symphony feel embarrassed, she felt like she had to do something to prevent the awkwardness but decided he needed to take ownership of being an asshole. Plus, Symphony knew the shit was about to blow through the fan.

"Aww, don't be like that, baby girl," Thomas said.

This time, Thomas looked down at Cash, who purposely hadn't looked up from his pie.

"Check this out, Cash! Look at this, Duck, pay attention. This is fourteen inches of titanium, and it's extra sharp. Set me back sixty-five dollars, but it can cut through a roasted pig like butter. Yeah, this is my new baby right here!" Thomas said, drooling over the knife.

Cash had a dumbfounded look on his charming face.

"What's wrong with you, boy?" asked Thomas.

Aunt Donna rumbled her throat.

"Why y'all so quiet!" Thomas said, looking around the room.

When Thomas laid his eyes on Steve, he froze. Thomas looked Steve up and down, and his eyes moved in slow motion, all the way down to Steve holding Elaine's hand. Thomas' face turned just as cranberry as Symphony's dress.

"Who the fuck are you?" Thomas said, looking at Steve like he broke into his house and peed on the floor.

All eyes turned to Steve, waiting for a good old-fashioned showdown right there in the dining room.

"Oh, Steve, this is my ex, Thomas, and this is his lovely girlfriend, Sonia, from Japan!" She pointed toward Sonia, who had a huge, genuine smile on her face.

"Hello, Steve!" said Sonia.

Thomas dramatically stabbed the roasted pig, and everybody jumped in their seats.

Thomas left the knife sticking straight up, in the pig's back, right smack in the middle of the table.

Everyone's eyes almost popped out on the table like ping-pong balls. Thomas mustered up a fake smile and extended his hand, walking toward Steve.

Everyone tensed up, not knowing what to expect. They all knew how Thomas felt about Elaine, but Sonia and Steve had no idea.

Thomas talked in a high-pitched voice to minimize the sense of a threat. Symphony looked back and caught Aunt Donna pouring an entire vodka bottle in the strawberry punch bowl on the high table. This party is about to get crazy, she thought and covered her face in embarrassment.

"Hi, Thomas. Nice to meet you," said Steve, sounding like a professional wrestler, his voice deep with a sort of a gargle behind his tone. They shook hands.

"Hey, man. How much do you bench?" Thomas put his hand on Steve's huge shoulder.

"About three fifty," he said, displaying how proud he was of himself.

Thomas shot Elaine an unreadable side-eye. Elaine didn't know what Thomas had in mind, but she planned to watch him closely, just in case he tried to pull a rabbit out of his sleeve.

"Hey, man, let's sit and have a beer," said Thomas.

"I don't drink," said Steve.

"It's OK. Donna, bring this man a drink please!"

Symphony gasped because when Tevah found Symphony passed out in the bathtub the last time she had alcohol, Aunt Donna was the one who mixed her drink. So Symphony felt sorry for Steve because Aunt Donna made alcoholic beverages that tasted like regular juice.

Thomas guided Steve to the main living area like he found his new best friend. Tevah laughed, watching Thomas suck in his round belly as he walked next to the buff, pale dude with jeans so tight that they had to be squeezing the sperm out of his balls.

"Here we go," Elaine muttered.

"*Everybody, meet me in the main family room for a game,*" *Tevah announced. Everyone migrated in the room and sat on the couches and wooden chairs against part of the wall, and some stood while the music played the song "Hey Ya" in the background from the rap duo OutKast.*

"*Who's ready to play the Family Trust Challenge?*" *Tevah announced.*

"*Everyone participating, please write your name down, fold it, and place it in this huge, empty wine glass on the table.*

"*Don't forget Steve!*" *said Thomas, handing Steve a glass of spiked red punch.*

❀ ❀ ❀

"**We're a tight** *family, right?*" *Tevah bawled with enthusiasm.*

The crowd shouted, "Yes!" But they hesitated as if Tevah asked them to jump off a mountain.

"*The point of the game is to show how much we, as a family, trust each other!*"

Tevah handed everyone a number, then shuffled up the folded papers with names in the glass. "So who has the number one?" asked Tevah.

Everyone shrugged looking around. Symphony opened the piece of paper. She raised her hand. "I'm number one."

"*Sym, pick a name out of the wine glass. Everyone, give Sym a hand!*" *said Tevah. The loud applause drowned out the music.*

Symphony picked the mini, square paper with

Cash's name.

"I got Duck!" said Sym.

Tevah and Symphony both knew Duck was in overprotective mode after their father disrespected Symphony at the dinner table. So Tevah played along with it.

"Sym, what you're going to do is fall back on the count of three, and I want you to trust that Duck will catch you. But with a blindfold on!" said Tevah.

Everyone laughed at the scared expression on Symphony's face.

Duck rubbed his hands together like he wanted revenge. "Remember that time you told Mom I had a girl in my room?" Duck whispered.

"Duck, if you drop me, I'll tell Mom some more stuff you did in your room, weed boy!"

Everyone laughed, including Duck.

"Oh, really?" asked Elaine, and she put her hand on her hip.

"I don't know what she's talking about, Mom," pleaded Duck.

Duck tied the blindfold in the back of Sym's head. He put two fingers near Symphony's nose.

"Now smell my fingers!" said Duck.

"Eww! Yuck!" Sym yelled. She swung to hit him but missed.

Everybody laughed.

Tevah positioned Symphony in the right way.

"Sym, you're going to fall back in one... two... three!"

Symphony fell back, and Duck caught her.

"What an adrenaline rush!" Sym shouted, and she hugged her brother.

When they got to player number ten, Steve raised his hand.

Out of all thirty-something people at the party, he picked Thomas's name.

Symphony felt immediately frightened. There was no way her father would let this guy Steve get away with stealing her mother, or so she thought.

Steve, on his third cup of spiked juice, said, "Come on, Thomas. Let's do this, man. I'll catch you! Hell yeah! Let's do this shit!"

"Steve, you picked my dad's name, which means my dad will catch you," Tevah corrected.

All the chatter stopped, and "Break Ya Neck" by Busta Rhymes blasted through the speakers. Steve's smile dropped.

"Oh, man," muttered Duck. "Maybe someone else should pick," Tevah suggested.

"I agree," Elaine said nervously.

"Come on, Steve. I got you, boy!" Thomas said excitedly.

Tevah shrugged. Steve waved at Elaine, telling her to stay back, "Elaine, stop. It's all good. Thomas is cool!"

Elaine couldn't take it. Steve's only known Thomas for five minutes, and now he's acting like they were best friends and future fishing buddies.

Steve turned and fist bumped Thomas.

"Alright. Get in position, gentlemen!" shouted Tevah, resembling a game-show host. She wrapped the *blindfold over Steve's eyes and maneuvered him into the position with his back a few feet in front of Thomas.*

Everyone pulled out their cell phones to record. The suspense filled the room. Symphony had the feeling it would be viral by the morning. Thomas opened up his arms out in the stance to catch Steve.

Symphony held her breath and searched Duck's eyes. Duck read her lips silently. "Would he?"

Duck deeply inhaled. "I don't know," he whispered.

Even the little children stopped and stared, and someone turned off the music.

"On the count of three, fall back, Steve," shouted Tevah.

"Got it!" Steve roared out like a WWE wrestler. Everybody shouted "One... two... three!"

Steve fell back at the exact moment Thomas sneezed, covered his nose, and moved to the side.

The toilet could be heard flushing in the distance.

Steve's huge body hit the floor so hard that the lamp fell off the end table near the kitchen.

"A damn bug flew in my nose! Did you see it?" Thomas proclaimed.

"That's fucked up," Duck whispered to Symphony while her mouth hung open.

Steve lifted his huge arm straight up, and he gave the thumbs up.

Laughter ripped through the silence. Somebody turned the music back on, and people were hunched over trying to catch their breath from what they just witnessed. Even Elaine had her mouth covered so soda didn't spray out.

"Just a normal day in the Dunmore house," said Cash. He snuck another look at Symphony. He loved the way her long hair swung over her eye when she laughed.

Thomas extended his arm to help Steve up.

"Man, you all alright?" he asked. Steve laid flat, lost in embarrassment.

"Who's next?" said Tevah nonchalantly. Sonia, Thomas's girlfriend, raised her hand and got Elaine's name on the paper. Sonia had a terrified expression. Mom had a devious smile.

"That's enough of the family challenge. I'm done!" said Tevah.

"Everybody, raise your glasses. Sym, congratulations on your college degree, and we want to wish you the best in your future endeavors! Cheers!"

"Cheers," the crowd echoed.

Steve stood, rubbing his back with his hand. "Man, Thomas, I'm starting to think you did that on purpose. I know she's your wife, but she said y'all are getting a divorce."

"What!" said Thomas enraged.

"Wait a minute. Thomas is not married," said Sonia in a soft voice. She looked around, and no one gave her eye contact.

"Bless your naïve heart, little girl," said Elaine. "Why didn't you tell me, Thomas? You have me around your family looking like your whore or some kind of mistress? Are you still sleeping with her?"

Sonia asked on the verge of tears. Elaine wanted some candy and nachos to watch this show.

"I'm sorry for hurting your feelings, but what I do with my wife is my business," said Thomas.

Sonia's eyes got bigger than speaker boxes. Her lips were a tight line.

"You bastard!" she said, raising her purse to attack Thomas.

"Little girl, if you hit my husband, they ain't gonna find your arms," Elaine threatened. Sonia put one hand on her chest appalled and marched out the front door.

"They don't call them rebound girls for nothing," said Aunt Donna, patting her afro, and taking a sip of punch.

"I'm out of here!" said Steve. Mom nodded, and he left.

"Dang, I forgot to welcome him to the family," said Tevah.

❋ ❋ ❋

"Oh my God, Tevah! I remember! Did Duck and I do the Kid and Play dance after that?"

"That's right! That's great, Sym! You're starting to remember!" Mom and Dad walk in the room while Tevah and I are watching our second movie in the living room.

My dad says, "Baby girl, don't you think you should get some rest?"

"No, Tommy. She needs some water," says Mom.

Tevah jumps in, "Sym, maybe you should wait a while before you move to L.A.. There'll be other jobs available. You should take some time to get your mind and thoughts together, especially since you had to cancel the wedding."

I look at them like they're a street gang about to fight me. I stand.

"I'm sick of all of you telling me what you think I should do. I'm twenty-two years old and don't need any of you to tell me anything!" I say, and I slam the magazine on the glass coffee table.

Crack!

I grab the keys and my jean jacket off the coat stand.

"Maybe she's hungry. Laney, get her something to eat," says Dad.

I stop and look back at Dad like he snatched my purse. "What? What's the matter with you?"

"Dad, that's not necessary. Why do you say stuff like that, especially right now?" Tevah says in irritation.

"Baby girl, don't go outside. Remember what the doctor…" is what I hear before I slam the front door behind me.

RIDES

*W**hy do they** insist on treating me like a child? I'm sick of it. I feel like I'm back in high school. Maybe if I set the garbage on fire in the backyard like Duck did or stole Mom's car like Tevah, I would've gotten more respect by now. I sigh. I push in the heavy, metal door. The back of the room is dark, and the front is lit up. The muggy humidity is warm when it touches my face, and the mixture of bleach, sweat, and rubber lingers. I know I'm in the right place because the little, blue car with the "Shake Something" sticker is parked outside. But where are the other cars? I look back at the dreary-blue sky. Maybe I should come back in the daytime. But something in me won't let me turn around. I pray to God that Bryson didn't pretend to have information to get a date. I gently close the door behind me. I don't know what information he has, but the suspense is enough to hold me captive in curiosity.*

The boombox in the right corner plays a hype rap song at mid-level. The air conditioner box in the window rattles hard like nuts and bolts hopping on the top of a spinning washing machine. I jolt back, gasping. That nearly scared me to death.

"Hello?" I say, trailing my fingers along the

cold, boxing rope in the center of the room. I pull out my keychain and squeeze the sanitizer in my hand.

There are at least ten red-and-black punching bags hanging from ten-inch chains. Some of them with small rips in need of repair. I spot the black speed bag against the wall on the darker side of the room. I've always wanted to hit one of those since watching the Rocky movies with Dad. It's like it's saying, *Come hit me now, Sym. Come smack the shit out of me.* I look around. The adrenaline quickly sets in, and now I stand before my opponent. Maybe I'll feel better after this. *Now, Sym, the doctor said a slip and fall is detrimental to your health so if you accidentally knock yourself out, you'll not only be embarrassed, but you'll be dead and embarrassed.* I ball my fists anyway. I raise my arm and swing hard. The bag flings back and forth, echoing through the room.

"Can I help you?" says the deep voice. I turn so quickly that I hear a snap in my neck.

Bryson's chest is lean and cut like he could punch somebody from here to Texas. My heart takes off. He has a gray towel around his waist and a black crowbar in his hand.

"I'm sorry. I'll leave." I head toward the door. There's no way I can outrun him, but my God I'll try. Tattoos cover half his body and wrap around his muscular arm.

"Rose?" he says.

I flip off the gray hood on my jean coat.

"Yeah. It's me, Rose." I swallow with my hand around the doorknob.

"I thought I locked the door. I didn't think you were coming. But I'm glad you did. Please don't leave," he says, pleading with his hands. I didn't know whether to run or stare. The sight of six concrete packs on his pan-flat stomach is freaking unreal. But the nervousness in my gut is way too strong to enjoy the visual.

"Alright, I'll stay," I whisper. I take a deep breath.

"Hold tight. I'll be back." He rushes off. Under his navel are tattoo symbols of VCR remote controller buttons. Okay, Sym—I mean, Rose. Your goal is to find out what happened to Popsicle. It doesn't matter what happens if you press the triangle play button. I found a seat on the weight bench near the ring. "So are you originally from Sacramento?" he yells from around the corner.

"Yes," I say, trying to shake out the visual of pressing play. "Did you go to Sacramento State College?" he yells from the backroom.

"Yes, I did."

"I knew there was something I liked about you!" I fold my arms.

"Oh, really?" He walks from around the corner with a white tee shirt and black sweatpants on. He's holding two orange sodas and a few mini bags of sweet-and-spicy chips with a black hoodie hanging on his arm. His aroma is strong, masculine, and deliciously fresh, like Irish Spring soap.

He passes me a soda and places his can on the weight bench next to me and sits. He pulls the black hoodie over his head, and I catch a quick glimpse of the triangle tattoo play button again. I look away to pretend I'm respecting his privacy.

His smile is warm and inviting. "A nice, wholesome college girl, huh?"

"Yes, that's me."

"I went to medical school myself but dropped out after the first year. I wasn't feeling it."

"An almost doctor, very impressive, Doctor B," I say, nodding. I press the cell phone screen, and he squeezes his eyelids from the flash. "I sent your picture to someone, just in case."

"Huh?"

"It's a safety precaution," I say, putting the phone back in my jean coat. "I thought I saw a flash at the cemetery, did you..."

"Umm, I tried to be discreet, but I forgot to turn off the flash. It's better to observe your surroundings right?"

"Hmph."

Hmph? What exactly does that mean? It's like he's having a meeting in his head about me.

"What do you mean 'hmph'?" I ask.

"Well, your security guard with the pink hair tried to end my life. Did you forget about that? I'm the one that should leave my clothes in the middle of the ring so the police dogs can sniff and find me, don't you think?"

Embarrassment forces my eyes to the ground.

"About that... My cousin is a little overprotective."

"A little?" He sighs in his sarcasm. He opens his can of soda and takes a drink.

"What exactly do the pink gloves mean on your sweatshirt?" He tugs on his shirt to look at what I'm pointing at.

"Yeah, I teach self-defense boxing for women. My friend and I came up with the concept in high school. When we got older, he opened up this gym, and I went to medical school. After I dropped out, I started teaching self-defense boxing out in Texas in a commercial gym."

"I bet it's like a man's dream being around women all day," I say, admiring the boxing ring.

He snickers.

"That may apply to some, but I have two major rules. I don't have sex with my students or women I work with. Believe me, they try, but I take my craft very seriously."

"Oh, a man with morals, not something I see often." There goes that tan toothpick in the corner of his mouth.

"Is that right?"

"What made you want to teach boxing?"

"Well, I used to get in a lot of fights in high school. My Aunt Minnie suggested I take up boxing to get my aggression out." He places a hand on the scruffy hairs on the side of his cheek.

"Aggression? Why were you so mad?" He hesitates a little.

"A lot of family stuff went on at the time."

"Sorry to hear that." I figure if he wants to share, he would tell me what happened with his family, so I don't ask. "What was your record back then?"

"Forty-two and zero."

"You must be pretty good?"

"Yeah. Good enough to get the job done." He licks his lips and plays with his tongue a little.

I look away. Did he just...?

"So umm, should I be scared of that aggression you speak of?" I squint.

"Depends. Some women like it." He chuckles when my eyes get big.

"I'm kidding. I know how to control myself, especially around a beautiful woman like yourself." His flirtatious eyes are studying me again.

As a matter of fact, Tevah stole Dad's truck twice. Not once, but twice and brought it back with a dent on the driver-side door. Dad took her phone for two days. What the hell is that about? Two freaking days?

"Are you okay? You look sort of ticked off." I shake out of my daze.

"Oh, sorry. Thank you for the compliment. I just have a lot on my mind."

"What's wrong?"

"Well, before I came, I got in a bit of an argument with my family. They treat me like I'm incapable of making the right decisions. Like I need them to hold my hand my entire life. Wait, why am I telling you this? Sorry, I didn't mean to—"

"Cold world. But it's not a problem at all. Are you the youngest in the family?"

"Yes, how did you—"

"Let me guess, all your life your family has played some part in fighting your battles?"

Well, there's Tevah. She beat up the prostitute we found in Todd's bed. Duck beat up bullies in high school. And people were too scared to come near me out in public because of Dad's intimidating appearance. And Mom still thinks I'm five.

"Yes. They've had some parts in handling some of the drama I've dealt with."

"Do you ever look at things from their point of view?"

"Why should I when I know for a fact I'm right?" I say coldly. I cross my legs and lean my weight against my arm that props me up—quite annoyed but focused.

"Well, do you think they hate you?" he asks.

"What? No, wh-why would you ask me that?" I stumble over my words.

"Only people who have some type of malice against you would lead you the wrong way on purpose, right? What about considering their advice for a second? You know, just a second to determine if you could even benefit from their opinion or not. Sometimes, we as people let our defenses block our blessings and opportunities because we're just plain ol' stubborn. You never know. There might be some good in what they're saying. Some people wish they had a family who cared enough, you know?"

How did he put things in perspective so damn fast?

"Well, that's something to think about. Thanks."

"Sure, little lady. It's not every day I get to talk to a beautiful, stubborn woman, especially one that puts a flower on the grave of a cat killer."

"You're never going to let it go are you?" I say in a chuckle.

"Nope!" He's stretching his arms.

"And I'm not that stubborn!"

"Hmph. So, tell me something. How long have you been putting flowers on those graves?"

"Not too long. But I try to go once a year."

"But why is it important to you?" he scratches his head.

"It's just something that I do. It's a place where I can go and think."

"Think, huh?" he says sarcastically. "My grandma Bonnie was buried there."

"I'm sorry to hear about your grandma. She must have been a lovely lady." I smile.

"Yes. She was," I say as convincingly as possible.

"So what made you choose to put a race car on Popsicle's grave and not the others? Was it a birthday present or something?"

"Birthday? No, there's no birth date on the tombstone, so I wouldn't know the birthday. I really don't know who Popsicle is."

Please don't let him be a part of the Italian mob. I could hear it now. *Drunk woman found on the roof one week, and two weeks later, found in a boxing gym, dead.*

"Oh, so you're stubborn and a bad liar," he says.

"Me, a liar? You're the one who had to lie to get a date."

"This is not a date, it's a snack." He tosses a small bag of chips without warning, and it brushes my arm and falls in my lap.

"Did you just throw a bag of chips at me?" I stand and point near his face.

"You throw another bag, and you'll be wearing chips. I promise you."

"Has anyone ever told you, you look delicious when you're mad?" he says, throwing me off.

"What am I, a full course meal," I ask in irritation.

"You can be if you want to be." He moves the toothpick to the other corner of his mouth with his tongue.

Three seconds go by, and I am speechless. *Did he just say he wanted to eat me?*

"C'mon, Rose, every year on March first, there's always a miniature car on Popsicle's grave. Was it you all these years? Today is the fifth year." I don't want to lie to him again. I already lied about my damn name, so I do what any twenty-two-year-old would do right now.

"Are you going to tell me about Popsicle or not?" I give him a "take it or leave it" attitude. He pulls a bag of Skittles out of his back pocket and pops a Skittle in his mouth.

"Popsicle is my mama." I blink slowly. "Your mother? How inconsiderate of me. I don't know how many times I mentioned her name—"

"Her actual name is Star."

"Star? What a gorgeous name. Again, I want to apologize for being so insensitive. I didn't know," I say, stumbling my words.

"No need to apologize. You didn't kill her."

My stomach somersaults and dives into shock juice. Did he say, kill? The fact that someone murdered Popsicle never came to mind. How could I ask? Would it be disrespectful to ask?

"Cancer. Cancer killed her." He takes a drink of his soda, staring off in space.

"Oh, no. I'm sorry. This must be hard for you."

"No, it's fine. What else you want to know?" he asks.

"Why was she called Popsicle?"

"Back when my daddy was alive, he said her thin, pale legs reminded him of two Popsicle sticks, and her red hair he said was the cherry-fla-vored kind. She also had faint, red lips. She mod-eled for a local advertisement clothing company back home in Texas from time to time. I know you think my accent's strong, but she would tell my daddy, *'I booked a lot of gigs with these legs, boy!'*" he says in exaggeration while imitating his mother.

He had sort of a glow when he spoke about her. He told me how Popsicle taught swimming in the summer and cooked collard greens and turkey necks on Fridays, which was also family movie night. She worked hard as a waitress to support them financially after his dad died.

I hated to hear that both his parents were deceased. I can't help but think if Popsicle needed to work as a waitress to support them financially, then how could she have afforded to pay fifty thousand a month for the After Wishes Foundation? Unless someone added her to their insurance policy.

"What was her personality like?" I ask, soaking up every word.

"She was in her mid-thirties and a free-spirit type of person before she died. Always dancing and singing. She thought she was hip too. One day, I was playing football outside with my middle-school friends. We walked into the house to get some water, and we all paused when we got to the kitchen. My mama was dancing and cooking while rapping Juvenile's 'Back That Azz Up' song.

"'Mama!'" I yelled. My mom spun around, eyes bulged out with earphones in her ears. Me and my friends fell out on the floor cackling. From that day on, they said I had the cool mom. She sang around the house all day long, and she loved mostly rap songs. My mama would say to my dad, 'Kevin, how do I sound?'

"And my daddy would say, 'Good, Popsicle. You sound real good,' as he sat in his beat-up recliner chair with the newspaper spread open. That's what I loved about my parents. They never tried to change each other."

Talking to Bryson is like pouring water, and I wanted to pour out my life and what happened to me just in the past week. But it's too much to deal with just meeting a person.

"Thank you for being so open with me, Bryson," I say. But I could tell there was so much more that happened in his life.

"So you're a girl who put flowers on the graves of strangers to make the world a less fucked-up place?"

"That's me," I say, tilting my head. He shows off his dimples with a grin.

"So you want to know anything else, Cheeks?"

"Cheeks? What cheeks?" I ask. He gives a quick nod and looks at my hips.

"My butt?" I reach over and hit his arm.

He says, "it's like a heart. Hmph. Is it all you?"

"What?"

"Come on, Cheeks. Why can't this boy catch a break? I answered all your questions." He pouts.

"Yes, I grew this butt!" I blurt out.

"Alright! That's what I'm talking about!"

"What kind of girls do you date, blow-up dolls," I ask sarcastically.

"Shoot, something like that, but let's just say, I'm trying something new. Rose, tell me something; why do so many trees got to die all because women want to use excessive amounts of toilet paper? And don't say because it's hard being a woman."

I gasp. "How about you answer this? Why do you men force respectable women to feel like they're not enough so much that they feel they have to pour a bottle of baby oil on their bodies in a bikini, then post it on social media because those are the only type of women you men choose to give attention to? And don't say it's because men like oil to jack off."

I couldn't hold a straight face. We both laugh. We laugh hard.

He looks back like he's listening to something on the boombox. The song "Permission" by Ro James is on. It's a mid-tempo R&B song. *With your permission, I want to spend a little time with you…*

"This is my favorite song," I say.

"No it's not," he says, raising an eyebrow.

"Yes it is, dammit!" He gets off the weight bench and jumps in the ring. He turns and pulls the ropes apart.

"If it was your favorite song, you should be dancing to it. Get in here, girl. This is my favorite song too."

"You don't want to do this. Can you even dance, Doctor B?"

"Come and find out, Cheeks."

The name Cheeks is beginning to grow on me. I think I like it, but I'm not going to tell him that.

I grip the rope and pull myself up. My foot slips. My heart leaps up my throat, and Bryson grips me tight underneath my arms. "I gotcha," he says, lifting me up. I climb in.

He has no idea how that slip could have turned deadly.

Looking down, I use my hand to straighten the wrinkles on my shirt. I look up, and he's in the middle of the ring with his arm up in the air extending his fingers into a rock-n-roll horn signal. He nods his head back and forth like he's in a rock 'n' roll concert, completely off beat from the music. I'm too terrified to move. *Did he forget that I'm standing right here?*

But then he transforms, and the Elvis *"uh-huh"* lip changes back to normal. I'm really confused now because he is now dancing to the beat.

"Come here." His voice is deep and provocative. He didn't ask me. It was like he commanded that I come. I'm hesitant, but curiosity overpowers my nervousness. I stand in front of him, and he takes my hand and twirls me. When I face him, I'm now an inch away. We sway side to side, and he taps my hip to the drums of the song.

"Scared you, didn't I?" he says with fresh-peppermint and orange-flavored breath.

"Uhh, yup." He places his hands on each side of my waist. I tense up.

"Is this too close?"

"No," I mutter. I slide my hands up the side of his hard biceps as he guides and controls my hips. We get closer with each rock. *Where did this swag come from?* His thigh brushes between my inner thighs as we dip and sway to the soulful drums. He bends his forehead, and it touches my forehead.

We are grinding so close that the warmth from his breath heats my neck. *What is happening right now?*

Tap, tap, tap.

His huge hands tap lower on my hips to the beat. He bites his bottom lip. His expression is serious. His greenish eyes search for something, but what? Are we dancing, or is this foreplay? I can't figure out the distinction.

"So why did you inquire about my hair earlier today?" I look up at him.

"Hmph... I'm the kind of guy who appreciates the things that other guys overlook. Like the shape of your collarbone for example." He slowly runs his fingers across my collarbone, barely touching it.

"So feminine and strong at the same time. And there's something so sexy and alluring about your hair."

"Thank you." He must have thrown that toothpick somewhere because it's gone.

He says, "What's on your mind?"

"I'm wondering what would happen if I press the play tattoo button on your stomach." Dammit, Sym. *Why did you ask him that?*

"Let's just say you'd better prepare yourself for a hell of a ride you ain't ever been on before."

"How would you know what kind of ride I've been on?"

"Because if that ride was any good, you wouldn't be here with me, dancing dirty, now would you?" He shows his perfectly white teeth, smirking grin.

"My mama used to say women love when a man knows a little something. So in my senior year of high school, I read every sex book I could find on how to pleasure a woman, and I bet I know your body better than you do."

"You think so?" I ask. "I know so."

"So I'm guessing you're in a relationship?" I ask.

"Not at all."

"Well, if you're not in a relationship, I guess you're not as good as you thought, Doctor B." I grin.

"Hmph." That last "hmph" sounded like a threat. I think I'm talking myself into some deep trouble. We sway from side to side. He clears his throat.

"What men fail to realize is it's all mental with women, and I'm pretty sure women prefer to be with someone that knows exactly how to push them over the edge."

He pulls me in closer. His cologne is a woody amber with a hint of vanilla, which heightens and ignites my sex drive. My lashes flutter, and the heat from his chest radiates lust surging down between my legs.

He continues, "All men have to do is educate themselves on the pressure points of a woman's body to increase the intensity to get them close to their peak, then take it away until the hunger builds up enough for them to beg for it."

His hands grip my jeans tight like he wants me bad, and his neck brushes up against my ear. His soothing, deep voice is possessing me into a relaxed state. The warmth of his hands caresses my back as my insides pulsate. I don't know why I let him do whatever he's doing, but I don't want him to stop. I'm speechless.

He continues, "Women hate it when men are silent. They want to know he's present, in more than one way. So men should whisper things like, you feel so good."

His tone is so deep and sensual directly in my ear. "Rose, you feel so good."

I'm celibate, dammit! I want to shout out.

My breaths are growing deeper by the minute. He reaches in his back pocket and pulls out the Skittles pack he had earlier. He uses the tip of his finger and slides it across my collarbone, moving my hair behind my back. Now I'm confused. He spreads out three Skittles on my collarbone. "Don't move," he demands.

The heat from his breath warms my skin, and his gentle lips scoop up each Skittle slowly. It's proactive, intoxicating, and dangerous. I now want Skittles for breakfast, lunch, dinner, and for a midnight snack. He slides a hand around my back and hugs me with the other. I wrap my arms around his neck and hold on tight as my insides contract into an uncontrollable burst, forcing my breath to shutter. I try everything I can to stop it, but the moan shoots out of my mouth before I cover it with my hand. *Did that just freaking happen? God, can I wrap him up and take him home with me?*

"It's amazing how I can have your body in this state and not have even kissed your lips yet."

"What state? I don't know what you're talking about," I whisper, still drunk in lust.

"Hmph." He snickers with a smile that says I'm not fooling anybody. I'm walking on dangerous ground here. This ride was minor but pleasurable. I can't imagine what it's like to go on the Bryson roller coaster.

"Do you usually dance with women you meet at cemeteries?"

"Not really. You're the first and the last. There's absolutely nowhere else I would rather be right now, Rose."

I want to tell him everything. I want to tell him about how I died and about how I ended up on the roof, but I can't. Our eyes find each other again. Another song comes on, but we dance to our own sensual pace. He studies me in silence, but something in his eyes tells me this isn't the last time I'm going to see him, like there's a potential future beyond tonight. I lay my head on his chest. I accept his gentle rubs on my back for what they are, comfort. He's nurturing my broken emotions, making it all better. He leans to the side, and he seductively dips me back like I'm a ballerina.

We both chortle to lighten the intense sexual thickness in the air.

"I have a talent," he says, looking down at me.

"Oh, yeah? What's that?"

"I'm a professional eye reader."

"Oh, really? So am I." I fold my arms.

"Ladies first," he says.

"I see a man who has endured so much pain in his life, but I can see that you're strong, and you live your life with great purpose."

"Hmph. You might be right." He clears his throat.

"I see fear. I'm not sure why, but if you get to know me, you'll see that I do want to hurt you, but not the way you think. I want to make you laugh so hard that your stomach tightens and your knees get weak, kind of hurt, ya know?"

"Why, thank you, Doctor B. That's the medicine I need right now. Positivity can go a long way."

"Oh, so I did good?" He has this hesitant smirk on his face with a mixture of arrogance.

"Honestly, yes. I must say that your prediction is pretty close, and I'll leave it at that," I mutter.

He moistens his lips. "Can I have a kiss?"

"Nope."

"Why not?" he says in a pouting manner.

"I don't kiss on the first date."

"Oh good, because it's not a date. It's a snack," he says. I push his chest slightly and bite my lip, trying not to smile.

"You're a lot different from the girls I usually meet."

"Why, because I don't do what you say?"

"Yeah, but I like it. Hmph. I'm glad you came, Cheeks." We hold each other, and he leans in closer, admiring my lips. Closer to kiss me. Closer.

Growl!

"Oh, my gosh! My stomach is so embarrassing!" I yell.

We laugh. We laugh hard. *Why are we laughing this hard? No, he didn't kiss me, but something tells me that won't be the last attempt.*

"So tell me, Cheeks, hypothetically speaking, if a hardworking guy like myself wanted to take you on a real date, would you go?" He squints at me curiously awaiting my response.

"Hypothetically speaking, it's a ninety percent chance that a nice, wholesome girl like myself would go on a date with you. But the percentage would be greater if you changed one little thing."

"What's that?" he says, frowning.

"Get rid of the 'Shake Something' sticker on the car!" He throws his head down.

"You saw it, huh?"

"Yup."

"That's my Aunt Minnie's car! It's the first car she ever bought in high school. She used to be on the dance team back then. I'm only in town for a few days, so I thought, why not? How about we meet at noon tomorrow, and I'll pick you up in my uncle's car from this decade?"

"I'll think about it," I say.

"Hmph. I make a mean frozen burrito. I got some in the back."

"Sure, I'll try it," I mutter. He helps me climb down from the boxing ring.

"Hold tight." He heads to the back, and I sit on the weight bench.

"You're going to love these! First, you gotta heat it up for two minutes, then put a thin layer of BBQ sauce and a slice of cheese on it, and pop it in for another minute in the microwave!" he says from the back room.

My phone vibrates and I answer, "Hello?"

"Symphony Dunmore, please."

"This is she."

"Hi, Symphony. This is Detective Mario Fields. I have some security footage from your neighbor across the street. It shows the suspect running from the side of your house the night of the party. I want you to come down to the precinct in the morning to view the footage. Look, I'm going to be straight with you. Symphony, your mother told me she doesn't know where you are. You need to know there's a possible suspect out there." My hands are trembling.

"Okay. I'll be there." I hang up. Bile creeps up my throat. I'm lightheaded. I take a deep breath.

Don't panic, Sym. I've got to get out of here. My stomach falls to my feet. *Did Bryson attack me? Maybe this entire snack-date thing is a setup? Has he been watching me for years?* Oh my God! *Why did I come?*

Bryson walks out the back with two plates of food. He stops when he sees my face.

"Rose, what's wrong?" he says, looking around the room.

Boom! The air conditioner knocks on. My breath is rapid.

"I gotta go!" I cry.

"Rose, what's wrong?" he says from the other side of the ring. I bolt toward the door.

"Stop! Leave me alone!" I scream. The tightness from my stomach throbs from my injury. I jump in the car. I drive off as the light shines through the open gym door.

PRECINCT

I **woke up at** *six this morning, and I haven't gotten out of bed. Tevah is a few feet away, snoring like a bear. I've never been so nervous to witness the sun light up the room. I would rather be snowed in than to meet with Detective Fields today, but unfortunately, it hasn't snowed on Mount Forty since—never. We usually get ready for massive thunderstorms that normally turn out to be sprinkles of rain.*

After I told Tevah what happened between Bryson and I last night, she almost dropped a tear in happiness. The mere fact that Bryson took control of my body commanding it to orgasm without even kissing my lips, in Tevah's words, is "next-level shit", and she asked where she could purchase a Bryson.

Is there really someone out there who wants me dead? Whoever this person is must look extremely suspicious to have been spotted on video. *Was it Bryson?* But I can't deny the mustard seed of doubt that still tells me I did this to myself.

There they go again. Mom and Dad are arguing downstairs. When the television is off, you can hear every word bubble clear unless you're behind closed doors in this house.

Dad growls, "Laney, that's not legitimate proof! After all this time, you still think this means anything? It means nothing! How many times do I need to say it?"

I wonder what kind of proof Mom has in her possession. We all knew Sonia was Dad's for-the-moment girl, and we couldn't blame him, because Mom treats him like monkey shit. But are they really going to divorce? I remember when Dad sat me, Duck, and Tevah down and swore he never cheated on Mom and even swore on the Bible. But Mom never believed him. They've been having the same argument for three years, and every time, it ends with him going back to his apartment and Mom walking around upset.

I get out of bed and shut the door.

That damn Bake-Bake-Bake show is taunting me. It's jumping like a rabbit on crack in my brain. Hi! My name is Betsie Sue, and I want to bake with you! The memory is pushing on the curtain in my thoughts but won't come out, and all it gives me is confusion in my gut, but why?

❋ ❋ ❋

I scoot back in the chair and take a deep breath. The burden weighs eighty pounds, and it's sitting in the middle of my shoulder blades. It's hard to look at my family because all their sad faces make me more anxious. The air is full of coffee beans, strong, flowery perfume, and fresh donuts. My father places a hand on the thigh of my olive dress, and my heel cap stops mid-tap on the hard floor.

"It's going to be alright, baby girl," Dad says.

I give a quick nod. We're sitting in the chairs against the mustard wall. Mom and Tevah are sitting on the other side of dad. With all the typing, ringing, and copy machines beeping, it certainly contributes to the pulsating migraine I have.

The formally dressed officers and detectives walk back and forth, some with gold badges hanging from their necks behind the receptionist desk. There is a huge window full of photos of missing men, women, and children on the corner wall in the waiting area.

"The detective will be out to see you in a few minutes," says the receptionist with the bifocal glasses.

I nod.

The detective called again this morning, stating he received some new information surrounding my case. At this point, everybody's a suspect. The man walking the German shepherd this morning, the mailman, and UPS driver. Everybody's a suspect. It's hard to function when I don't know if I'm to blame or someone else. On top of it all, I ran out of the boxing gym like a tempestuous lunatic. Bryson probably thought Freddy Krueger was after me. I'm sure, by now, he thinks I'm crazy. But it's too late now, and I doubt I'll ever run into him again. All the miniature cars from the After Wishes Foundation are gone now, and I bet someone at the After Wishes Foundation must have known Bryson and I would meet, but why like that? Which reminds me... *Why didn't I ask about the cars?* Well, of course I didn't plan to run out like I did. I guess I'll never know now.

Since we've been here, Tevah hung up on somebody four times. I would love to feel a sense of normalcy right now. I straighten up in my seat again and rest my sweaty hands on my lap.

"Mom, Dad, Tevah, I'm sorry for snapping on you last night. I didn't mean to break the glass on the table, Mom," I say.

"No need to apologize. I understand. You're going through so much right now. I'm just glad that God brought you back to me... to us," Mom says, reaching over Dad's lap to touch my hand.

"It's alright, baby girl." says Dad.

"It's fine, Sym," says Tevah. I sigh in relief.

"Thanks."

I stand up and sit next to Tevah. "Who keeps calling you?" I whisper through the fifty conversations going on behind the receptionist desk.

"It's nothing," says Tevah, scratching her arm. I sharpen my lips.

"Do you want me to tell Dad somebody's harassing you? Spit it out."

"It's Todd. He's been calling since we left the cemetery yesterday."

"What? That's who you were hanging up on?"

"Yeah."

"He says he needed to talk to you. He wants to

still give you the wedding of your dreams, blah, blah, blah. But I told him to buck-off. Not fuck off, but buck-off."

"Buck-off?" I ask.

"Yeah, I didn't want to curse."

"Oh, I see. I have no idea how he ever got your number!"

"He probably paid to get my number with one of those stolen credit cards from his old clients," she says.

As if paying a twenty-thousand-dollar escort wasn't bad enough... I just thank God for the warning.

A short woman walks in, and her little girl has the cutest ribbons in her hair.

❋ ❋ ❋

Five-year-old Sym

I remembered how my beads click-clacked when I watched Dad turn the corner with the lady with the pink hair and tiny, pink robe.

"I'll be back," said Dad.

The Bake-Bake-Bake show blasted through the little apartment. I scooted back on that ugly, purple couch, unzipped my backpack, and used my pencil to draw the pizza on the television, and then I drew myself as a stick figure eating it.

"Hi! My name is Betsie Sue, and I want to bake with you!" said Betsie Sue on the television.

I knew something was wrong, and after sitting there for a while alone, I heard a woman faintly scream over the show music. Almost like she needed help. What was my father doing to her? Even the music from the Betsy Sue show couldn't drown out the woman making all those funny noises through the thin, white walls behind me. My hands trembled so hard I could barely stick my fingers in my ears. I had a yucky stomach ache. I didn't like the way it made me feel. I had to find Dad.

I did exactly what my father didn't want me to do —I got up to find him. As soon as I turned into the hallway, I saw the brunette lady with the pink highlights follow my dad in the next room across the hall, and the light flicked on. I remembered feeling terrified of getting in trouble, but I had been sitting there so long, and I hated waiting. The door was slightly cracked open. My father stood next to the lady. His palm tree shirt was buttoned wrong, and his black slacks were disheveled, and he had the lady's hand? Holding it?

He gazed in the lady's eyes. "I'm sorry," he said.

"Hey there, little girl. Did you miss your daddy? You stop that crying," my father said. But he wasn't talking to me. He was talking to the baby girl with the same peach skin, brown eyes, and smile as him.

"No, that's my daddy!" I cried.

They both gasped and looked my way, and he dropped the lady's hand.

"Hey, baby girl. That's right. I'm your daddy. Let's go, baby!" He looks at the lady with a serious expression. "I'm sorry, I can't come back here." The woman took the baby out of his arms with watery eyes.

"Symphony, Daddy will get you whatever you

want! How about another chocolate milkshake?" he said in a chipper voice.

"Okay," I said in a whisper, and I stopped crying.

"Daddy, where's your paperwork?" I said when he got in on the driver's side of his truck.

"Oh, I'll get it next time. I had to fix her toilet instead, but do me a favor, if your mother asks, don't tell her we came here. Your mother doesn't like me fixing other people's toilets."

"I won't tell her, Daddy." That day, he promised to take the family to Disneyland.

A year later, after Bible study, everyone stood around chatting. The lady in the back of the sanctuary looked familiar. She stood in the back with a stylish, pink suit on, and her hair was still brown with pink highlights, but this time, the baby was old enough to walk on her own. I never noticed her before. We missed the morning service and attended the noon service, which is something we never did. I saw my father headed her way. I knew my mom would be furious if she knew Dad fixed that lady's toilet, but when he got close to her, he walked right past her like he never saw her at all.

I heard my mother whisper to Aunt Donna, "That lady with the pink hair, the guys in school used to call her a baton." Aunt Donna laughed. Baton? I thought. I had no idea what a baton was, but I'd listened to them talk and found out a baton had something to do with how the lady with the pink hair hung around a lot of the men in the church. But little did my mom know "the baton" had been around my dad too. I couldn't *stomach watching another episode of Bestie Sue's baking show after school anymore because it always reminded me of the girl that tried to take my daddy from me.*

❋ ❋ ❋

Detective Mario Fields is walking in our direction, blowing his nose with a tissue. His gray suit is oversized, and he's walking with huge strides between the desks.

I slowly turn my head and scowl at my father. How could he? This is the man who raised me to never let a man disrespect me, yet he's the same man who fathered a love child that we knew nothing about. *And to add insult to injury, he took me, little five-year-old me, to the apartment of his mistress? Why haven't I thought of this before?* He knew I was way too young to understand back then, but I understand now.

Dad squints suspiciously. "You alright, baby girl?"

"Hi, Symphony. Nice to see you again," says the detective.

But I don't speak because I'm too busy studying my father. He has a stern look of concern on his face, probably about my well-being. *Is he faking it? Does he really care?* My father is an actor. He's done this same look a thousand times with my mother. I know it all too well. He knows exactly how to manipulate. He has perfected the look of deception and is accustomed to a double life. This is the man who swore on the Bible in front of his children that he would never cheat on Mom. He convinced us that Mom was delusional. This is the man who lied to all of us, and I'm pissed upon pissed right now.

"Detective Fields." I swallow.

I extend my arm to shake the detective's hand.

"Symphony, you okay?" asks Mom.

"Yeah," I force out.

"First, what we're going to do is bring you back to the office and ask you some questions, and then, if we need your family, we will come and get them."

"I understand," I mutter, still in disgust with my father.

THE INTERROGATION ROOM

*A*s soon as *we walk in, I see the huge, rectangular mirror on the wall of the small room and a tiny, black camera on the ceiling in the corner. I sit down on the black, plastic chair, and the detective sits on the other side of the wooden table. He opens the manila folder and flips through it.*

"So first things first. How are you, Symphony?"

"I've had better days."

"Is your memory still sketchy?" His demeanor is straightforward.

"Unfortunately. I still can't remember what happened to me."

He clears his throat. "If I can direct your attention to the television please." There is a mini television, probably twenty years old, on the roller cart. He picks up the remote control and points it at the TV. An image of what appears to be my house is on the screen but without color. The entire house looks dark gray, especially the area outside my bedroom window. There are people walking around in the front yard, and there are a mixture of dark and light grays, but it's hard to see their faces.

"I want you to take a look at this surveillance video. My partner spotted a person running from the side of your house, but when I watched the video, I saw the same person hanging with party-goers much later. We no longer have suspicion to think he did something to you. I have something different to show you. This is from your neighbor, Mrs. Wallace, diagonally across the street. Some-how the wind pushed her surveillance camera out of position, and it focused on your house. She kept a camera inside the panda bear bush on top of her fountain."

Oh, really? I wouldn't be surprised if she did that on purpose after Tevah stole the postal truck when we were younger.

He coughs on his fist, then presses fast for-ward on the remote. "We don't have audio, but we may have a possible lead based on the visual." He presses play, and it plays back to normal speed. "Okay, at this point, people are going in and out the front door, but there's something that stands out," he says.

At this point in the video, nobody's outside. A skinny dude in dark clothing knocks on the front door. A big, husky guy opens it. The husky guy looks like my brother, but the video quality is fuzzy. The husky guy grabs the skinny dude by his arm and leads him to the driveway on the side of the parked cars. They exchange words, almost like they're yelling because they're pointing in each other's faces. The husky guy pushes the skinny dude, and they both look down like something fell out of someone's pocket. They exchange words again, and the skinny dude picks up whatever fell and tosses it at the big guy. He catches it, and the skinny guy walks off. The husky guy sticks his hand in his pocket, looks both ways, then goes back in the house.

"Who are these two guys?" asks Detective Fields.

Wait, was that Todd?

"It looks like my ex-fiancé, Todd, came to the party, and my brother told him to leave. So he probably told him to stay away from me or something. Wait... Tevah told me she shut the door in his face, so he must have come back after that," I say.

Detective Fields folds his arm on his big, round belly. "Yeah, that makes sense. But things took an interesting turn this morning." He rubs his forehead.

"I talked to your brother, Patrick—well, Duck, as everyone calls him—and he had some interesting things to say, but it wasn't about Todd; it was about Cash. Symphony, I'll just be straight with you. Your brother says Cash attacked you."

I blurt out, "Duck said what?" I jump out of my chair. "Why would he say that? That's not true!"

The detective scratches the back of his head.

"I asked myself the same thing. Apparently, Cash hired an expensive defense attorney to get your brother out of jail from that hospital fight, so I'm hoping you can make sense out of all this."

The confusion spins around my head like a wheel.

"Detective Fields, my brother, and Cash are very good friends. Cash grew up across the street from us. I'm sure there must be some kind of mistake—"

"No mistake at all," he interrupts.

Duck, come on, bro. You're not giving me much to work with here. What the hell is going on? Now Duck is blaming Cash? Why?

A woman knocks on the door. The detective opens it, and she hands him a huge box. He sits it on the table in front of me. He places the items one by one on the table. First, a leopard pen, a thick cutout of the carpet, a gold wrapper, and my purple cell phone.

"We obtained these items from your room. Do any of these things look familiar to you?" he says. "Do any of these items bring back any memories? They were found on the ground in your room in front of your dresser."

The tan carpet has specks of brown smudges the size of quarters—one after the other in a straight line to the edge.

"Oh my God! Is that my blood?" I push fear right back down my throat.

"Yes."

"I don't see how any of these can help right now, Detective."

"Wait right here. I'll be back, Symphony."

When he comes back into the room, Mom, Dad, and Tevah follow behind him, and he shuts the door.

"Do any of these items look familiar to you?" he says, looking around at us.

"I bought you that leopard pen!" says Mom, pointing. I pick up and observe the leopard pen.

"Oh, yeah. That's right. My mom bought me this. It is a recorder. She gave it to me the day before the party. I'm a celebrity news correspondent —well, I will be when I get to L.A.. I have a job waiting for me out there. When I use it, I hold the pen like a microphone and record myself in the mirror to work on my technique."

"Symphony, do you mind if I turn on the recordings?"

"Go ahead," I say.

"I'll be right back." He picks up the pen and leaves the room. What's up with this guy? He's acting like he's on to something. He comes back ten minutes later, and he looks like he's hiding something because he's avoiding eye contact with me.

"What's going on?" I say in concern.

"Symphony, you're not going to like this," Detective Fields says, shaking his head in shame. Now I'm officially about to shatter in a thousand pieces, and I don't know why.

"Symphony, I'm going to play this for you and

your family." The leopard pen clicks when he pushes down on it.

❊ ❊ ❊

Bell Biv Devoe's "Poison" *faintly plays.*

"Hi. My name is Symphony Dunmore, and I'm here to bring you the latest celebrity news! No, Sym. Say it with more enthusiasm. I'm here to bring you the latest celebrity news!

"Now I sound like a game-show host. "Big Don Love is back at it again, and guess what? Baby number ten is on the way with baby mama number ten! Ladies, this is an example for all of us to always use protection! Don't sleep with these men because they're rich, because guess what? You can get your own money! Shoot, I drank too much champagne. Ugh!"

"Oh my God! You scared me. I didn't hear you come in."

"How's it going," asked a man with a deep voice.

"Practicing for my new job, but I'll be downstairs in a few minutes."

"That's my dude, working hard, even at your own party?"

"That's Duck," Tevah blurts out.

The detective covers his mouth with a finger for Tevah to be quiet.

"You always stay so focused. That's what I love about you," Duck said, slurring his words.

"Thanks, bro! Your eyes are crazy red. You okay?"

"Forget about my eyes. Dude, are you fucking

Cash? I saw him come downstairs. Was he in your room?"

"Duck, why are you asking me this? So what if he was? It's my room."

"So you can be with a loser like Todd, then be some groupie slut for Cash? Cash didn't even want to take you to prom. I had to give him my guitar for him to go with you. So you're one of his fucking groupies now? Dude, you don't fucking listen!" Duck hollered as loud as he could..

"Oh my God, you're serious? Duck, you're freaking scaring me! Get the fuck out of my room, now!"

"Todd told me everything. You've been fucking around with Cash this entire time! I knew it! I fucking knew it!"

"Duck, stay away from me." The metal clicks. The door must have gotten stuck again.

"You just don't get it, Ronnie!"

"Duck, stop!" I grunt, and it sounded like a bag of clothes were thrown to the ground.

"Tu'ua o ia!" said a woman's voice, sounding flustered.

"Who's there?" Duck said, sounding shook.

There was no response.

The music plays, 'Twinkle Twinkle Little Star...'

"Oh, shit!" He sniffs hard.

"Where did these fucking balloons come from? Dude! Oh my God, Sym! Wake up, wake up," said Duck in a panic. The dragging noise resembled a couch being pushed across the carpet.

Click clack!

A swift scraping, like a wooden drawer is being opened, or a window? Now it sounds like someone is dragging a garbage bag full of books, or something equally as heavy and awkward. There's that scraping drawer noise again.

Click clack!

Pop!

"Oh, shit. Why would a balloon pop right now? I need to get the fuck out of here," said Duck, stumbling his words.

The "Cupid Shuffle" song is loud. A door slammed, and the music muffles.

❋ ❋ ❋

The detective pulls up a chair in front of me.

"Symphony, do you understand what we just heard."

"Yes," I whisper. "Some guy attacked me at my own party." But it's like my emotions can't comprehend what this means. The detective crosses his fingers.

"Symphony, it wasn't some guy. It was your brother. Your brother did this to you."

"What, wait?" I say, jumping up. I distinctly remember hearing a woman's voice too... And he called me Ronnie...

Dad speaks slowly on the verge of tears, "The woman said, *'tuʻua o ia'*, which means 'leave her alone' in the Samoan language. It sounded like my mother, your grandma Bonnie."

"See, my brother would never do something

like this, and you better not try to pin this on him! Wait… Grandma?"

Dad nods. "Detective, how is that possible? She passed away," he stutters, constantly shaking his head in disbelief. "See, Detective, this proves my point. Someone else was in that room! It couldn't possibly be my grandma," I say, pointing with each word. I shoot him a vicious stare. "And another thing—" The hand grips my shoulder.

It's Mom. "Your brother did this," she says, searching into my eyes.

"What?" I say. Tevah wraps her arm around mine with wetness forming in her eyes.

I look at Dad. I've never witnessed beaming rage igniting from a human being at that magnitude before.

"But what did he hit her with," asks Tevah. I swallow.

"He hit me with the Gold Bubbles Champagne bottle. I put it on my dresser when Cash came to my room earlier that day," I mutter, staring off in space.

"Sym, you remember," shouts Tevah.

"Yes, now I do. He picked up the bottle like a bat and swung." My voice is slightly above a whisper.

My dad scratches his head and gets eye contact with the detective. He says, "Duck just came home from the army. He was stationed in Iraq. Do you think something happened out there to have caused him to lash out like this?"

"No, Mr. Dunmore. If he was active duty, that would have showed up on his record. It does not. There's no record of him being in the army at all."

Mom says, "are you telling me that Patrick never joined the army?"

"That's correct, Mrs. Dunmore." I want to walk out.

This is too much. I hear this, but am I really comprehending this?

"Detective Fields, why are the memories coming back now?" I say in confusion.

The detective held up a finger. "I think I know the answer. The police report shows that eighteen years ago, you witnessed a little girl fly out the front car windshield. You went into some type of panic attack, and then a few minutes later, you had no recollection of what happened. You were about five back then. Did Symphony see a medical professional about that?" asks the detective, looking back and forth at Mom and Dad.

"No, sir," says Mom. Detective Fields raises both eyebrows.

"What! I witnessed something traumatic, and you didn't get me checked out!?" No one is looking at me, not even Tevah.

"Patrick had a tough life before he came into your lives. You never know what sort of things kids go through, you know what I mean," says the detective.

"What are you talking about?" I ask.

"Symphony, you do know that Patrick is

adopted, right," asks the detective.

"What? No! My parents would have told me!" I look back and forth between Mom and Dad. My mom says, "Duck called you Ronnie… His biological mother's name is Ronnie…"

"I'm sorry. I thought you knew. This is something usually discussed by the parents. I do apologize that you had to find out this way," says the detective.

"I want to go home," I blurt out. Detective Fields stands and opens the door.

"You're free to go." Oh my God! My brother tried to kill me? I look at the linoleum floor. How can I go to Los Angeles like this? I want to eat Red Vines on my bed and stay locked in the guestroom indefinitely.

DISASTER

*I*t's been sixteen *minutes since I found out my brother did the unthinkable, and I don't know how to feel. My brother is the same man who taught me how to hold my hands to clap. He's protected me my entire life. It's almost like how they clean the skin with rubbing alcohol before giving a lethal injection. Why would he protect me only to kill me? We walk out the precinct doors, and I see two detectives standing on the cement platform near the steps holding coffee cups.*

"Yeah, that's him. They never found the body," says the female cop, looking out into the parking lot.

"You know what they say: 'no body, no case.' He probably chopped him up and fed him to the dogs," says the formally dressed male cop. He snickers.

I wonder if he had a good laugh about my case too. *Jerk.* They are looking directly at several men standing on the side of a black Mercedes. The detectives walk into two different directions.

The parking lot is the size of two small gas stations, and there isn't anyone else nearby in the direction of the guys by the Mercedes. One guy is wearing a white shirt with predominantly broad shoulders and blue jeans. Another guy has on all black, and the older gentleman looks sort of like Billy D. Williams. They're standing around, listening to someone talk on a speakerphone. *Cash? Is that Cash in all black?* We reach the bottom of cemented stairs.

Why would those police officers make those accusations looking in Cash's direction?

"There's Cash," says Tevah.

"Yup, I see him." Cash sticks the cell in his back pocket. His chest slumps in. Just when I think this moment can't get any worse—Cash starts coming this way, and the guy next to him resembles Bryson. *It is Bryson. My Bryson... "not a date but a snack" Bryson? Is this really my life right now?*

I don't have room to take on anything else on my plate. It's full of disappointment with a dash of lies. Bryson's eyes catch mine. There is pure confusion in his eyes, and I stand firm so I don't pass out.

"I just got off the phone with Detective Fields," says Cash. Cash squeezes me tight in our embrace. He holds me tight. I'm numb. I don't know what to feel. "This is crazy. I never thought he was capable of doing something like this," says Cash.

Yup.

"Yeah, this is in fact crazy," I say.

It's almost as crazy as my best friend treating me like a stranger after I got out of the hospital and then showing up with a guy I embarrassed myself in front of the night before.

Bryson's gaze is of discomfort and bewilderment. "Sym, this is my dad, Fred, and my cousin, Bryson," says Cash. I catch an inkling of confusion in Bryson's face when he hears the name Sym and not Rose.

Did he say Bryson's his cousin? And I always thought the guy with Cash's mom was his dad.

"I'm sorry to be meeting you under these circumstances." Bryson reaches out, and I shake his hand. He's so hard to read right now.

"But it's nice to meet you," says Bryson.

"Thanks." I nod.

"I've heard so much about you. God will see you through this," says Cash's dad.

"Thanks," I mutter. I hate for Bryson to see me in this vulnerable state, but it's not like I have a choice. But in this moment, I want nothing more than to put my head on Bryson's chest so he can make it all better. I want him to tell me I will be alright. Bryson is the only one here who knows how to soften the blow. Everyone veers toward the commotion, and Cash clinches his jaws.

My legs are toilet paper.

"That's my sister! That's my sister!" hollers Duck.

Two officers are escorting him from the far-right corner of the building. He's wearing an orange jumpsuit, and his hands are in handcuffs behind his back. Everything moves in slow motion. Duck headbutts one officer and knocks the other against the police car window with his shoulder. The officer's body hits the concrete along with the explosion of glass, and Duck is running in my direction.

Cash stands in front of me and slightly pushes me behind in a ready-to-attack stance. I am torn. Torn between the love for my brother and terrified at the same time.

"Tommy, no!" yells Mom. My father is running full force toward Duck and derails the three-hundred-pound train of Duck.

"Don't you ever touch my daughter, mother fucker! I'll kill yah!" My father hit Duck's face so hard with his fist that I thought Duck's head would fly off. Blood oozes out Duck's nose. Duck tries to shove Dad with his shoulder but misses. Dad wraps his hands around Duck's throat, and he turns lily white. Duck kicks and misses with his cuffed hands behind his back. Out of nowhere, Bryson is able to maneuver my dad's hands from Duck's neck while three uniformed cops forcibly pull Duck to the ground and lay him flat on his stomach. Bryson is talking to my dad with his arm around Dad's shoulder, trying to refrain him from going back for more. I don't know what Bryson says to Dad, but my dad's brick fists open up.

Screeching tires and sirens scream, surrounding the scene. More officers run from the side of the dirty-gray building.

Detective Fields charges out the front office doors with other officers just as my father barges back to us. The cop smashes my brother's cheek to the pavement with his shoe.

Duck hollers, "I'm sorry, Mom! Sym! Tevah! I didn't know something was wrong with me! Cash, stay away from my sister, man!" Duck's voice is between a threat and a plea.

Cash stares him down.

"You fucked up, bro. Get help!" Duck has a smug expression right before the cop pushes him in the back seat.

Detective Fields says, "I apologize, folks. I thought you folks were long gone. A new officer took him out of the holding cell way too soon."

Detective Fields whispers something to Dad.

Bryson walks straight to the black Mercedes, opens the passenger door, gets in, and slams the door.

It must be too much for him like it is for me right now. Todd knew my brother was overprotective. He never believed Cash and I had a platonic relationship.

Todd knew my brother would overreact and probably try to fight Cash and ruin my party, but instead, Duck attacked me. Todd could have seen Cash with Duck before the party from his mother's house. I knew Duck was controlling, but this took things to a new, twisted level. But why? It doesn't make sense.

On the way home, Tevah and I are in the back seat of Mom's Camry while Dad drives, and Mom sits on the passenger side.

I lean over and whisper, "Tevah, I found a therapist, and I authorized my doctor to send my medical records to the new hospital. The only catch is… the therapist and hospital are in Los Angeles."

"What do you mean? I canceled our flight when you were in the hospital. And when did you have time to do all this?"

"This morning, on my phone."

"Sym, you're not thinking clearly."

"I don't care. I want to get the hell out of town as soon as possible."

GUILTY TRUTHS

*W**e walk in** the house from the garage. We just made it home from the precinct. The clunking of shoes on the wooden floor and unzipping of coats fill the air in the main living area. I'm numb. My body doesn't know how to accept such a horrific betrayal, and something in me will not allow me to feel. How am I supposed to feel when the one man who protected me was the same man who tried to kill me? The thought is like swallowing a bowling ball of disbelief.*

Dad helps Mom take off her white peacoat and hangs it on the brass coat rack. Anticipation and a hint of what's not being said circulates through the thick silence.

I sit on the couch and grab a cushion to rest my arms. Tevah sits next to me. Her eyes are red from crying. I rest my elbow against the arm of the couch. I lightly touch my stitches on the side of my head. They don't hurt as bad anymore. Mom and Dad sit on the long couch with pain on their faces. Dad shakes his head in shame, breathing heavily. He leans forward with his elbows on his knees. Mom is staring off in space, and her posture is straight up with her legs leaning to the side.

I have so many questions bouncing around in my mind. I want to know why they didn't tell me Duck was adopted. I don't feel like it would change how I feel about my brother, but I have to know why. And why would dad bring me to his mistress' house, and why didn't my parents ever take me to a doctor for my memory loss.

"Grandma Bonnie must be your guardian angel, Symphony. We heard her voice as clear as the sky," says Dad, focusing on the ground. "Boy, I miss my mother."

Tevah says, "Dad, what did the detective whisper to you?"

"They searched Duck's car and found a gold wine bottle with blood on the bottom." I'm holding my breath.

A vision covers my sight. *I was around fifteen maybe, sitting in the back seat, and Mom is stopped at a red light. Tevah looks back at me from the passenger side, then Mom.*

"Symphony, what did you see, dammit," shouted Mom.

I blow out. Mom clears her throat. "We tried to conceive for months before we had you. But then I got sick. Chunks of my hair fell out, and my pants size went from a seventeen to a three. My arms were too weak to cook, I had no appetite to eat, and I remember being too sad to produce tears. By far, the toughest year of my life, but your father helped me through it," she says, looking at Dad. "I got tired of feeling like some human science experiment with all the different tests the doctors had me do. So I prayed to God and said, 'Lord, if You want me to go to Heaven, I will go, but if You want me to stay here on Earth, please heal me in Your name, Jesus.'" She looks at the ceiling.

This must be why Mom is so germaphobic. When we were kids, she never let us leave the house without a bottle of sanitizer.

Mom rubs her hands together.

"I had the doctor cancel all my future appointments. After that year, I got my appetite back and started gaining my weight back, but the doctors thought it was still too risky for us to conceive children. So we adopted a five-year-old boy named Patrick."

"Why didn't you tell me when you told Tevah?" I ask.

"Well, Tevah was helping me organize my closet, and she found the adoption papers. But I told her not to say anything."

Dad sucks his teeth. "When Patrick walked through those doors, he became a Dunmore, and there was nothing anyone could say to change that. I'm not making excuses, but both his parents were drug addicts, so he may have been exposed to things we don't know about. I know this a lot for you, maybe you should stay home a while until you're one-hundred percent healed. There'll be other jobs out there, baby girl. It's a lot for one person to deal with."

Even if I knew Duck was adopted, it certainly would not have changed the way I loved my brother, but they never gave me the option to decide for myself how I felt about it. I'd always had to fight for my respect around here to prove I was actually a responsible adult. News flash, people! I'm twenty-two years old! I sigh. I have to tell them. I say, "Mom, Dad, we're driving to L.A. in the morning."

"What? Why so soon?" they blurt out, looking at Tevah for validation.

"Yup," says Tevah.

"I can't let this situation beat me. I can't. I won't, not now." I stand.

"Mom, Dad, yes I'm scared to be out in the world, and yes, I admit I struggle with anxiety from time to time, but I want you to know that there's no way I'm going to stop taking care of myself. I need you both to trust me. God gave me a second chance for a reason, and it's time for me to take on the next phase of my life. Dad, I want you to trust that I won't fall back into eating irresponsibly. Mom, I want you to know that you have prepared me to take care of the maintenance that comes with being a woman. You two have prepared me for this moment my entire life. I don't want you to worry about something going horribly wrong in the next chapter. I'll be fine. Just know that I plan to live my best life to the fullest and with no regrets."

"That's my baby girl, all grown up. I'm sorry for all the fat jokes. I was only trying to help," says

Dad.

"Uhh, okay, thanks," I say, tightening my lips. I look over at Mom.

"I know you know how to wash your own clothes, Symphony. I just feel weird not having little kids in the house, that's all," says Mom.

"Mom, it's cool. I'm sure one day Tevah will bring you a couple of grandbabies to babysit."

"What!" Tevah says, frowning.

Dad says, "You are a grown, mature woman, and we wish you the best. We wish you both the best in whatever you want to do."

I kiss my dad on the cheek. I lean down to hug Mom, and she pulls my arm toward her. Her arms are squeezing the life out of me.

"Kind of tight, Mom," I struggle to say. "No, really. I can't breathe." She lets go of me and snickers through her tears.

Dad says, "Baby girl, I want to take the time to acknowledge something. If I had taken the time to fix your bedroom door knob weeks ago when you asked me to, maybe you would have gotten away. I'm so sorry. I know I make a lot of promises, but I'll do better going forward. I want to apologize to you all."

Mom looks surprised. "Wow, Tommy. We've been married over thirty years, and you finally admit to being a procrastinator. Good for you," says Mom.

Dad shoots her an inquisitive look. "Now, Laney, I told you to take Symphony to get checked out after that accident. You know good and well I was too busy."

"Oh, so you're blaming me? So, you been busy for eighteen years, huh?" She tilts her head and leans back on the cushion.

"Stop it!" I yell.

"You two sound like children! I'm not wasting any more of my life listening to this arguing shit! I'm the one that got knocked the fuck over the head with a bottle and died! You need something significant to argue about? Dad, how about you tell Mom about the secret love child you had with that lady with the brown and pink hair! Yeah, you made Mom look delusional when you have another daughter out there in the world. Yeah, I remember now! And Mom, how about you... How about you..." I couldn't say it.

My lips are stuck like glue. I couldn't say it. *Oh my God! I remember. How could she? My mother is a freaking monster.*

Mom looks at Dad like he tattooed *sinner* on his forehead. I wait for him to deny it all, but Dad won't look at her, and his eyes are staring at the wooden floor like he's trying to conjure up a good explanation.

I march off, and Tevah follows.

Grandma Bonnie's old room door is wide open. Tevah and I go up the stairs. I stop and look back at Tevah.

"Grandma didn't die in her sleep, did she?" I whisper.

Tevah's eyes are as wide as plates. Her eyes tell me everything, and she knew exactly what I meant.

YEAR THREE OF THREE WITH GRANDMA

*P*ure shock is *still on Tevah's face after I told her what I remember about Dad and his mistress. We both find it insane for him to make us doubt Mom the past three years, just to cover up his lies. But the vision that covered my eyes downstairs is horrendously cruel, evil, and awful.*

Tevah sits on the bed, and I stand to pace the room back and forth.

"Tevah, I just had a vision of Mom mixing poison with Grandma's orange juice when she was alive."

Tevah is curiously eyeing me.

"Sym, give me a play-by-play of what you think happened to Grandma Bonnie the day she died."

"*That day, I remember being irritated because Grandma Bonnie called my cell phone before the alarm buzzed to wake me up for school. I unraveled my twisted braids, threw on my purple sweatshirt, and walked downstairs. Dad had already left early that day, because someone got hurt at the construction site. Duck had already left to work at the taco spot, and Mom pushed us to hurry, because she was on a set schedule to volunteer at the church after she dropped us off at school.*

"So that left a fifteen-minute window that Grandma would be by herself until Aunt Donna arrived after working her midnight shift. I remember wondering why Grandma was up so early, because she normally slept during our morning routine. This time, she was propped up with a bunch of pillows behind her back and alert, and her heavy breathing resembled someone snoring while awake. And I can't forget that humongous picture of Cesare Borgia hanging over Grandma Bonnie's headboard watching our every move. Tevah, you had your backpack on by the nightstand next to Grandma. I think your hair was purple that day, and I remember it being all cut to your shoulders. You poured out two pill tablets from the bottle into the mini white cup and put it next to the water bottle on the nightstand. Mom set the spinach omelet, wheat toast, and fruit on the food tray connected to the bed, while I swept up the crackers that Grandma Bonnie spilled from the night before.

"Grandma said, with her strong, Samoan accent, 'Maybe you should find a job instead of forcing my son to take care of you.' She looked directly at Mom and rubbed her thick arms.

"I stopped sweeping and looked at Grandma Bon-

nie like she left her mind in the bathroom. Mom wiped her hands over the fresh white sheets that she washed and folded, so that Aunt Donna could change Grandma's sheets when she got there. Mom remained calm and continued to set up the room like she did every morning for three years, and acted like she didn't hear what Grandma said.

"Grandma said, 'My son should never have married you. You can't even cook. Humph!'

"Mom dug the tip of her fingernails into her thumb.

"I told Grandma not to talk to my mother that way.

"Mom said, 'Symphony, no!'

"I remember you saying, 'How about we starve her old ass for a few days.'

"'Tevah, hush up,' Mom said before she left the room.

"'Symphony, come here, dear. When you get older, you must straighten your hair to get a job, so the people will accept you better,' Grandma demanded.

"Tevah, you stood next to the nightstand, mumbling something under your breath, and you were still holding the fuzzy pink duster.

"'Grandma, no disrespect, but why would I change who I am, and what I look like to please someone else?' I said.'

"She coughed. 'That's how the world works. They help people more who look like them, dear.'

"Mom came back into the room with a glass of orange juice and placed it on the food tray."

"'And you, you're not a good mother. Why would

you let your daughter get fat? Your daughter's fat. She'll never get a man. Symphony's fat.' Grandma laughed through her congested breath.

"*I remember thinking, 'Why would she say that about me?'*

"*At that moment, my heart took off running down the street like I knew something bad would happen. But Mom was hard to read through the calmness she gave off when she walked back in the room.*

"*'Symphony, baby, go in the kitchen. There should be one more waffle left with your name on it. I'm going to finish up before we go,' Mom said.*

"*'Fat, fat!' Grandma said with a laugh and examined my body as I walked out all flustered. And that's when I saw Mom sprinkle some white powder in Grandma's orange juice.*

"*'You too, Tevah. Go in the kitchen,' said Mom.*

"*Tevah, you said, 'Yes, ma'am' and left the room, too.*

"*'What did you say about my daughter?' echoed off the walls of the silent house. It was so quiet that Mom's voice sounded like she was still next to me in the kitchen.*

"*I remember wondering why Grandma would say those things about me. And for her to laugh, cut deep. Real deep. I was fifteen then, but why would she take things so far? I thought. I already had to deal with being called 'the chunky girl with a pretty face' at school, and now I had to deal with this kind of issue at home? And I wondered if Grandma purposely tried to torture me with her words? Or was it about torturing*

Mom?

"Grandma laughed, then said, 'I say she's fa—!' Her condescending tone stopped abruptly followed by a gargle.

"The hair on the back of my neck sprouted up like bristles from a brush.

"Next thing I remember is being in the back of the car, crying hysterically, and I had no idea why."

❋ ❋ ❋

My black dress slightly raises on my thigh as I slide down the cold wall. I am now sitting on the carpet. I cross my legs. I'm staring at Tevah, hoping she could put this puzzle together. Tevah leans against the bedpost.

"So one minute, Grandma's calling me fat, and the next minute, I'm in the back of Mom's car, crying. What am I missing, Tevah? Something's missing, I can feel it."

Tevah hesitates. "Sym, just leave it alone," she says like it's no big deal.

I get up. "Tevah, stop hiding things from me, and don't think I'm not pissed about you keeping Duck's adoption away from me. I want to know. I *have* to know. What happened?"

Tevah stands in front of me and puts a hand on both of my shoulders. She sighs. "Think about it, Sym. After Mom asked Grandma Bonnie what she said, what did you do?"

"I don't remember."

"Think about it harder, Sym. We were all

upset. Think about it."

"Wait a minute… I walked back into the room, didn't I? And you never came back in the kitchen."

"Sym, close your eyes. What do you see? What do you feel?"

I close my eyelids. "I remember feeling scared. I remember feeling angry. I walked in the room, and I see you with your arms folded by the nightstand watching something."

"Where's Mom, Sym? What is she doing?" asks Tevah.

"Mom is… Mom is… sitting on top of Grandma's stomach like a saddle with her hands around Grandma Bonnie's neck? Grandma Bonnie's arms are waving all over, and she's gasping for air. And her legs are bent, jerking back and forth in a struggle."

"Oh my God! Mom killed Grandma?" My eyes slowly open. I walk next to the bed and sit.

Tevah sits next to me. "Tevah, how can you be so calm about this?"

"Sym, think about it. What happened after you saw Mom do that?"

I force myself to remember. *Come on, Sym, I tell myself.*

I remember how Grandma's arms dropped. Mom climbed off of her and stood on the side of the bed.

All three of us stood around staring at Grandma Bonnie's lifeless body. The bathroom fan swooshed around, and I heard a car drive by.

❋ ❋ ❋

Mom cried out, "See what you made me do, you awful, old lady! Lord, forgive me! Oh, God! What am I going to do? I snapped!"

"Maybe we should call the police," I suggested. I knew there was only a matter of time before I fainted.

"Hell, nah! If we call the police, Mom will go to jail," Tevah said, breathing hard with nervous eyes.

"Wait a minute... Tevah, check her pulse," muttered Mom.

"No way! Not me!" Tevah's eyebrows sunk in. "Sym, you check her!"

"Who, me?" I pointed at myself with eyes bulged out. I slowly walked closer to the bed. As soon as I reached to touch Grandma Bonnie's wrist, she coughed, and my heart spilled out to the floor.

"Lord, how am I going to get out of this?" asked Mom.

"You, bitch! You tried to kill me! I can't wait to tell my son!" Grandma strained through each cough.

"Lord, help me," Mom muttered.

"Help! Police! Leoleo! Police!" Grandma hollered hysterical through each cough. Suddenly, she stopped and laughed. An evil laugh.

The maroon curtains swayed violently back and forth. The floor viciously shook. I ran and held on to the doorframe, Mom held the thick bedpost, and Tevah hit her shoulder on the closet door before she grabbed the doorframe. Grandma Bonnie's eyes rapidly look left and right in fear.

"It's an earthquake!" said Mom.

Suddenly, the shaking ceased, and our petrified eyes searched frantically around the room.

Grandma Bonnie broke the silence. "My son is going to leave you, bitch..."

Snap!

Creak!

Grandma Bonnie looked straight up to the ceiling. The huge, fifty-pound picture frame of the fake Jesus crashed directly into Grandma Bonnie's neck. The massive crunch killed every instinct of speculation that she could have survived. And the eyeball that rolled next to my shoe turned me into a block of ice.

Mom jolted back with praying hands in front of her mouth. "Jesus, Yahweh, my Lord!"

"God helped you, Mom. I guess He was listening," I said, stuttering between my rapid breaths.

Tevah peeled off her backpack, unzipped it, and pulled out her cell phone. "It's 7:40 A.M. Aunt Donna's going to be here in ten minutes! Let's get out of here, now," she said in a panic.

Mom wrapped her hand around my wrist and pulled me to the kitchen. Mom grabbed her purse off the counter.

"Where's your backpack, Symphony? Go get it," Mom said.

"But Mom..."

"Now!"

I took my backpack off the dining room chair and followed Mom and Tevah through the kitchen door into the garage.

We backed out the driveway as the neighbors

started coming out of their houses looking left to right. They were probably discombobulated from the earthquake.

The gospel song "We Fall Down" played on the radio in Mom's car.

We stop at the red light.

Tears fell down my eyes like a rainstorm.

"Calm down, Symphony!" said Mom, looking back at me.

"Sym, stop!" said Tevah.

"What?" I asked.

I felt confused. I wiped my tears, not having any idea as to why tears came down my face. I was so confused when I saw their frightened faces looking back at me in the car.

"Sym, what did you see?" asked Mom.

"What?" I looked at Mom like she was going nuts.

"Symphony, what did you see, dammit!?" yelled Mom.

"Mom, what are you talking about?" I said, wiping the tears from my face.

"Mom's talking about how Grandma normally pretends to be asleep when we go in her room in the morning," said Tevah nonchalantly.

"Oh, yeah. Grandma probably does that so she doesn't have to say thank you. She just had to be up this morning to make sure we did everything right. That's what I saw, Mom, didn't you?" I asked.

"Yeah, your grandma is so bossy. That lady is a lot to handle. Bless her heart," said Mom.

REALITY

"**S** **o that's everything** I can remember," I say.
Tevah scoots up to the edge of the bed.

"Sym, something happened. You had no recollection of Mom choking Grandma or the earthquake or the picture frame crashing onto Grandma Bonnie. One minute, you were freaked out, and the next minute, the memory was gone. Mom told me not to talk to you about it. That's not something she wanted you to remember. Hell, I wish I could forget. So when Dad sat us down and told us that Aunt Donna found Grandma deceased in the bed that morning and that she died in her sleep, you believed it. Dad made up a lie to protect us from the horrible truth. Grandma Bonnie died from a freak accident. It's like the memory hid somewhere in your mind. Somehow you assumed she went to sleep after we left."

"Oh my God! Why would they not take me to a psychologist? Who does that? And Mom must have known that I would forget, just like the accident I witnessed when I was a kid. But how could she have been so sure?"

"I don't know, but she wanted to protect you, Sym. Protect you from the truth." Anxiety creeps up my spine.

"I can't blame Mom for what she did before the freak accident. Grandma Bonnie scrutinized her for years. She was bound to snap," I say.

"Tevah, how can you be so cool about this? You were around sixteen, and you saw someone die."

"The same day that Grandma died, I went into the girl's locker room and vomited all the waffles I ate that morning. I thought about it for weeks and fell into a deep depression and saw a therapist but kept the true reason for my depression to myself. Knowing you were okay gave me comfort. I can't lie, I wish I could forget. I looked up some stuff online on how and why you may have forgotten what happened. I think the doctor was right. I think you have Dissociative Amnesia."

I sigh. "That sounds about right. I wonder if all this could have contributed to the anxiety I had. When I think about it, I've been burying things my entire life. I knew Todd wasn't the right guy to marry, but I buried my emotions and was going to marry him anyway. I pretended like he was the perfect guy, ignoring all the warning signs for the sake of having a dream wedding. *But at what cost? Why would I waste my time?* Time I could never get back but certainly an experience I could learn from. This explains why I would feel sad with no explanation of why. My conscience shut off what

I really saw, but I still experienced the sting of affliction, suffering, and agony in my gut."

"I'm sorry, sister. I know you have a lot on your mind, but if it means anything, I will never keep another secret away from you, ever."

I nod. I never knew my life could be surrounded by so many lies. I've been around so many deceitful things that it baffles me that all this time it's been hidden above in my own mind.

I laugh. I laugh so hard my shoulders shake from the chuckles. My stomach tightens, and my head throbs a little from my stitches.

"Sym, why are you laughing?" Tevah asks, looking at me like I popped a few happy pills in my mouth.

"Daddy has an illegitimate love child, Mom choked Grandma, and Grandma came back from the dead to stop Duck from finishing me off. Not to mention, I met the guy of my dreams, but I can never date him because he's Cash's cousin, and that would make me a total slut. This shit is hilarious! Don't you think?"

I inhale and exhale a whistle to settle down.

MILKSHAKES

*T*evah *went downstairs, and I'm sitting at the foot of the bed staring at it as it taunts me. Dad got the biggest size available. It's a double-blended, chocolate milkshake with fluffy, cocaine-white cream on top, and it's holding up the cherry like a trophy. Certainly an addiction that once haunted me to tears.*

If my dad knew about the blood, sweat, and pain I suffered to break away from my sweetest bad habit, he would not have been so willing to bring a chocolate milkshake to put a smile on my face. *But guilt can make people do the strangest things, right?*

Why is it that forbidden things look so tasty and suddenly become the very thing you need to survive on earth? Hmmm… like Bryson. But I know that drinking this would plummet the unrelenting stress I feel building up in my chest. *Why would Duck try to kill me?*

Drinking this will soothe me, but only for the moment. I call it my antidepressant. I've been in this moment at least a thousand times to know that when the last drop is consumed, I will hate myself. *But hell, this is an emergency, you know what I mean?* But I care too much about my life to relapse and moonwalk back to the chocolate-milk-shake girl again, who they once called the chunky girl with the pretty face. Jerks.

I pick up the emergency salt shakers, and I stand before my past addiction. I remove the lid and shake and shake until I can't shake anymore and watch the whip cream trickle down the side of the foam cup. I take off the straw wrapper and use the straw to slightly stir. I plug the top of straw with my thumb and pull it out to hold the chocolate inside. It drizzles back in the cup, and it's cold on my tongue. The salty chocolate is so disgusting. I spit it back into the cup. Shit. Sorry, taste buds. Now that should trigger a friendly reminder to my brain that I despise chocolate milk-shakes. Mission accomplished.

I take out my pants from the laundry basket, fold them, and put them in the open, black suitcase on my bed. My shoulders jump at the knock on the door.

"Come in."

"Hey, Symphony. Someone's here to see you," says Mom.

"Who?"

"It's Cash. Listen, Symphony, I don't completely understand what you got going with Cash, but getting into another relationship this quick may not be a good idea. You never know, y'all might be together later on in life. And of course I would love for you to be with a rich and handsome guy, but I remember my first boyfriend was young, rich, and handsome—well, rich back in my day meant having a refrigerator full of food, but that's beside the point.

"My ex-boyfriend had the nerve to call me to bail him out after he went to jail for slapping the girl he was seeing behind my back. Well, all I'm trying to say is look for warning signs, and pay attention."

"You're right, Mom. I know I can be a hopeless romantic sometimes." I roll my eyes.

Mom places her hand on my forehead. "You got a fever, baby?" she says in concern.

"No, Mom. I agree with you, that's all. It's not like you hate me. I know you're just looking out for me." I scrunch my eyebrows.

"Naw, baby. I don't hate you. Well, okay then." Mom grabs the doorknob.

"Mom, I'm sorry for bringing up Dad's other child like that. Well, I guess she would be my sister, but it had to be said."

"Symphony, I don't want you to worry about that, and for the record, I already knew."

"Mom, how did you know?"

"I'll show you." Mom leaves the room and comes back with a folded piece of paper.

"I got this from your drawing book when you were five."

She passes it to me. I unfold it, and it's a colored crayon drawing of stick figures of our immediate family standing in a row on green grass with a bright-blue sky and a one-story house in the back. I'm a stick figure with huge, puffy pigtails with long lashes, Duck with short, curly, black hair, Tevah with brown hair to her shoulders, Mom with a red hairband holding Daddy's hand while Daddy is kissing a pink-haired, stick-figure lady as she held a baby close to her chest.

"Oh, wow," I mutter.

"Sym, I found this three years ago in the middle of spring cleaning."

"This must be the paper you shoved in Dad's face the day you ran Dad over in front of the house?"

"Yes. He deserved it too."

"Mom, Dad still loves you. Are you going to divorce him and run off with Steve or something?"

"Right now, I'm not sure. But I feel our family should start the healing process of what happened to you before tackling anything else. In a sense, it made us stronger. And nothing's going on with Steve. I used Steve to get back at your father. I wanted him to slowly suffer alone, not to go get a girlfriend. Besides, Steve is my fitness trainer. I thought I told you. I bought a mother-of-the-bride dress for your wedding a few sizes too small. You never know, I still might need it in the future, so maybe I should keep Steve around."

"Mom, Dad's going to flip," I say sarcastically.

"There's absolutely nothing going on with

that hunk of a man, Symphony. I don't want you to worry about me and your father. He's been here every day, and I even let him keep his key to the house, for now." She winks.

"Mom, do you believe in guardian angels? Do you think that was Grandma Bonnie's voice on the voice recording who scared Duck off?"

"I don't know. I pray every night for God to protect our family, so I wouldn't be surprised if God sent someone to protect you, even if it was your grandmother."

I don't tell her I remember how Grandma Bonnie died. I know she's already worried about me leaving for L.A., so I don't want to make things worse, especially now that I'm going on with my plans.

"How's Dad? Is he mad at me for telling you about his secret daughter? That was tacky of me to tell you at that moment. You know me… I like to be in control. I kind of lost it. I'm sorry."

"Naw, your dad knows he was wrong for exposing you to that kind of thing. Taking you around some mistress was dumb and had to have been confusing to you. But he's somewhat relieved that you forced him to tell me everything."

"But Mom, why stay married to him knowing he has an extra kid?"

"Symphony, when I think about the thirty years of love and our family, it supersedes the mistakes that we both made in our marriage. But only time will tell."

"Yeah, only time will tell," I repeat.

"Go ahead and pack. I'll go get Cash from downstairs. Your father is probably talking his ear off about those cutting knives again. Oh, and I'll be sure to send you on your way to L.A. with a sweet potato pie, Symphony. I mean, Sym." She snickers.

I smirk. Mom's trying to display the respect I've been asking for all this time. Sweet.

"Actually, Mom, you can call me Symphony."

"Thanks, I would love that," she says.

"Oh, Mom, do we have family in Texas?"

"No. Why?"

"Oh, never mind. It's nothing." Since Popsicle was from Texas, I thought I would ask. Now I'm convinced I'll never find out why I was chosen to put those cars on Popsicle's grave. Mom looks suspicious, then walks out the door.

SHOT CLOCK

A ***few minutes later,*** *Cash knocks on the open door. "Hello, anybody home?" He has a look of concern, and he's a little hesitant.*

"Come in, stranger," I say, cuffing my socks and placing them in the suitcase on the bed.

Why does he have to look so good? His arm and chest muscles slightly push up against his Gucci dress shirt. *Why does he have to smell like lust?* Damn those cologne companies. His rough hand slides around my back, and we embrace. *What woman wouldn't want a wealthy, talented man who squeezes you like he's about to leave the country?* But just because he possesses all these qualities doesn't mean we were meant to be or that we have to be together. I can't forget the gold music box that I never got in that Snoopy box. Not getting the music box is a clear indication that it's certainly not our time to be together. One thing's for sure, he's not leaving this room without answering some questions. This time, I'm going to take my time being alone, and honestly, I'll probably never trust a man again, thanks to Duck. Plus, I like Cash as my best friend—well, that's still up for debate, but I must admit, he usually plays that role very well. He sits down next to my suitcase. His expression is serious. "How are you holding up?"

"I'm fine, but I think I'm in shock."

He observes the suitcases on my bed. "Are you going somewhere?"

"Yup, Tevah and I are driving to Los Angeles in the morning."

He's looking at me like I said I'm rocketing to the moon. "Already? Really?"

"Yup. I'm seriously leaving," I say, lifting both eyebrows. "That's a six-hour drive. How about you two come with me on my private jet? It's scheduled to leave tomorrow at ten in the morning."

"No thanks, Cash."

"Come on, Sym. I'll make sure you have everything you need, including Red Vines and a warm blanket. I can even hire a masseuse or give you a massage with my own two hands," he says with a smirk.

But I'm not falling for it, not this time.

"Cash, why did you rush off the phone with me after I got out of the hospital? And you never came to check on me."

His convincing demeanor turns into seriousness.

"Sym, I told the cops I was the last person with you. Someone at the party found out and posted it on social media. People started calling me a woman beater. An advertiser pulled out of a multimillion-dollar contract deal when they saw the rumors lingering online. They told me it wasn't a good look for the company or some shit like that. So when you called, my lawyers were going over hypothetical scenarios of what could happen if I was charged with assault or attempted murder, so they told me to get off the phone, and advised me not to go near you. I'm sorry, Sym. I didn't know what to do."

"Oh, I see." I don't think he realizes what he is saying. This is the second time he chose his career over me. The first time, he moved to New York and barely said goodbye. This time, he left me hanging when I needed him the most. Yet I'm the same person he says he's in love with. I'm the same person whose name is tattooed on his chest right now, and I am the same person who almost compromised my intuition for another man. We were supposed to remain friends. But I'll take it as a lesson learned. I will never compromise myself for another human being again.

He stands in front of me and wraps his hands gently around my hand, staring deep in my eyes. "I love you, Sym, and I hope we can get past this together. I feel like we belong together. You never know. Maybe one day we'll have five kids running around or something." He shoots me a gorgeous smile to lighten up my now tensely folded arms.

"Most likely not." I slip my hand out of his grasp to turn around.

"Cash, I have to pack." I reach behind the suitcase to grab another shirt to fold, but the hand on my hip startles me a bit. I turn around. Cash is standing right in front of me.

"Please forgive me, Sym. I should have been there for you. I fucked up. I didn't know what to do."

Cash presses his pillow-soft lips against mine. His finger tickles my cheek as he guides my wavy hair to the side of my face. I back up a little. *I knew it. I'm flabbergasted. I felt absolutely nothing in his kiss. How did I have an entire make-out session with him the night of the party and feel nothing right now? The alcohol. The dirty freaking alcohol must have played a major role. Relief swirls around my chest.*

"Cash, I'm not ready. I want to focus on me and my career."

"Wait. Are you throwing me back into the friend zone right now?" he whispers.

I shoot him my business, no-nonsense eyes.

"Sym, you've been through so much these past two weeks. I want you to know that I'm here for you, and I'm willing to wait and do as much as I can to make it up to you. Until then, I can only hope God sends a message from me to penetrate your heart."

"Cash, you're amazing, but I don't want you to wait for me. I've wanted nothing more than to be a celebrity news anchor. I can't fully focus on my career consciously knowing you're waiting. That's not what I want."

He's holding both my hands.

He sighs heavily. "I understand." He leans down to kiss me again. I look up at him and stop him with my hand on his hard chest. "Just friends, Cash."

"Yes, friends," he mumbles sarcastically. I grab some pink underwear out of the basket to fold.

"Let me fold those!" He tries to take the underwear.

"Damn, you're tempting!" I laugh.

"No, Cash."

"Hey, Cash, I don't recall you telling me about your cousin Bryson before."

"Oh, yeah. He's a cool, laidback kind of guy. His aunt Minnie is married to my dad. Remember when we were younger how I would be gone for most of the summer? I was at my dad's house in the city. Bryson's mom fell on hard times financially back in Texas, so when he was thirteen, Aunt Popsicle sent Bryson to live with my stepmom and dad."

Cash hasn't mentioned anything about me and Bryson's snack date? Why didn't Bryson tell him? It's definitely not a can of fluffy worms I want to open.

"So did it take his mom a while to get things together?" I ask.

"Well, actually, my aunt Popsicle died. She saved up money from her waitress job and had gotten approved for an apartment down the street from my dad's place. Her flight was set to leave at night, so a few hours before, she stopped by her job for a small going-away party that her co-workers put together. Shortly after they cut the cake, they found Aunt Popsicle passed out in the kitchen. She later died at the hospital."

I gasp. "So sorry to hear that. Cancer is taking so many lives every day," I say.

He squints suspiciously.

Shoot, I think I just outed Bryson because Popsicle having cancer is not something I'm supposed to know.

But then he says, "Cancer? No, she didn't die from cancer. Have you heard of secondary drowning?"

"No," I say. I don't know what his point is, but my ears are perking up.

"It's when water enters the lungs, causing inflammation and it makes it hard to breathe, which causes a condition called pulmonary edema. Normally, when we take a breath, our lungs fill up with air, but with this condition, they fill up with fluid instead. But it usually takes twenty-four hours for someone to show signs like coughing or a fever. Also, people can get affected when water gets into their lungs from swimming."

The tears fight to be seen, but I push them back.

"Wow," I whisper.

Maybe Bryson kept that from me for the same reason I didn't give him my name. Too private to share.

"Very heartbreaking," I say.

"They found your aunt at her own going-away party unconscious like you guys found me?" I say.

"Yeah. I actually told the nurse to make sure fluid wasn't in your lungs when we got to the hospital that night because the situation was so similar."

I say, "did Popsicle go swimming somewhere?"

"Actually, no one knows, but it was winter." *How could the worst day of my life be so close to Popsicle's worst day? And there's no way I can let what happened to me hold me back from what I'd been working so hard for, not right now. I know I'll have to deal with what happened, but not today, I don't want to. I'm still numb. This is my second chance, and I'm pushing on for me, and I'm pushing on for Popsicle.*

"Cash, downtown at the precinct, I overheard two cops talking and looking in your direction. Allegedly, you, Bryson, or your dad may have chopped up a body and fed it to some dogs?" I look at him like snot oozed from his eyes.

"That's tough. Sort of sounds like a movie." He snickers.

His lips vibrate when he blows out air. "Sorry. I've been busy touring. I don't have any time to chop up anybody."

"What about Bryson?" I ask.

"Bryson... he's a low-key kind of guy. He's only been in town a few days to support me because I thought I was going to prison. So there's no way Bryson had time to visit his mom's grave and chop up a body. And sorry, my dad doesn't have a dog."

He laughs.

"Not funny, Cash." I scowl at him.

I guess I'll never know what those cops were talking about. One thing's for sure, Cash isn't a killer, and I felt so safe with Bryson at the boxing gym before I got the call.

"So did Bryson already know who I was at the precinct?"

"Not exactly. You blocked me from all your social media accounts a long time ago, so I showed him the photo we took at your senior prom."

My mouth fell open. "You did what?"

"I carry it in my wallet everywhere I go." He pulls the Gucci wallet out of his back pocket and pulls out the mini prom photo.

"Cash, I looked like a shiny, blue hippopotamus!" This must be why Bryson didn't recognize me at the cemetery, I thought.

"You looked beautiful to me… still do," he says with flirtatious eyes.

"So is it true? Did Duck give you his guitar for you to go to prom with me? Is that what you wanted to tell me the night of the party before you stormed out of my room?"

"Sym, it's not what you think."

"Tell me, Cash. What am I supposed to think?"

"Sym, I fell in love with you on your prom night. I don't give a fuck about that guitar."

"Do you still have it?" I raise my eyebrow.

"Yes, Sym. But you mean more to me than some guitar. Don't you see that?" He pulls out his iPhone from his back pocket and begins to text somebody.

"Who are you texting?"

He's focused on typing on his phone. "You don't believe me. So I have to work twice as hard to tell you how I feel."

I poke out my lips, staring at the word bullshit written in the orange bubble caption over his head. His phone beeps.

"What about now?" he says.

He shows me his phone. It's a video of a recording studio with microphones and stands, a mega-engineering board, grand piano, and a set of drums. A guy appears on the screen holding a red electric guitar. He then starts swinging the guitar on the ground until it breaks into five wooden pieces and broken string.

Cash says, "You still think I care about that guitar more than you?" I cross my arms.

"I guess that's a start to earn my friendship back," I say.

"What's so special about the guitar anyway?" I ask.

"Prince used it in his rehearsal at his last concert. His manager carried in a new electric guitar, and Duck was working security and caught him before he threw away his old guitar."

"Prince? Is that what Duck told you? Sorry to burst your musical balls, but Duck never did security at a Prince concert, and I doubt Prince would have touched an old twenty-dollar guitar from the friendly neighborhood garage sale from down the street. I'm the one that told him to pull over so I could check out a bookshelf. I was there when he bought it."

"That muthafucker. That's tough." I giggle, and my head throbs around my stitches.

"On a serious note, I wonder why they didn't have a record of Duck being in the army. I'm sure he'll be in jail for a long time now," I say. Confusion is the only emotion I have, because I don't know whether to love or hate my brother. I'm torn, and I think I still may be in shock.

"Sym, I can't stand here and lie to you. Duck didn't go to the army. I paid for him to seek treatment at a rehabilitation center for drug and alcohol abuse, but after a few months, he thought he was cured and left the program."

"What? You have got to be kidding me."

"I wish I was. That's why I didn't want you to marry Todd. He's the one that gave Duck drugs. It made him spiral out of control. Duck never did speed until Todd gave him some free drugs when they met... I guess to get in good with Duck."

"Oh my God! I got to tell my mom and dad." Cash has this weird look on his face. "They already know. I told them downstairs."

"Wow! Nobody tells me anything around here! I guess that explains why Duck came back home after only a few months from the military."

"So is that why Duck didn't fight Todd at my party? I saw surveillance of them the night of the party in front of the house arguing. It looks like Todd dropped something, and Duck picked up something and put it in his pocket." My heart rapidly thumps.

"Cash, why didn't you tell me?"

"I didn't know he left the treatment facility until I showed up at the party to surprise you. He didn't want me to say anything. He wanted to tell you himself."

I press in my temples on the sides of my eyes.

"Let's change the subject. This is too much," I say. Cash sticks his hands in my basket and picks up my blue lace panties and starts playing with it.

"So what do you say, Sym? You and Tevah can ride in the jet with me. There's plenty of room. It's only a forty-five-minute flight compared to your six-hour drive. Plus, we both know you don't want Tevah to drive. You drive like an old granny, and she drives like a jewelry thief." I punch him on the arm and grab my underwear.

"Cash, I think Tevah wants to have a 'sister-cousin road-trip' thing—"

He twirls my underwear on his finger.

"Nope, Tevah already put in an order for steak and potatoes. I talked to her downstairs." He smiles.

I shake my head. She set me up. I sigh.

"What time should we be ready?"

"I'll send a car by eight."

"Sym, are you expecting company? I saw this girl outside sitting in a red buggy. She's parked in front of my mom's house, but she keeps looking at your house. She's been out there for a while. A little weird."

"Thanks, Cash. I think I know exactly who she is."

DAISIES

I *t is eight A.M. The cool breeze blows my bangs, and the wind stings my eyes. The Cadillac limousine is parked in front of the house. The driver is wearing a black suit, red tie, and a chauffeur's hat. He's loading up the trunk with suitcases from the porch. Cash had some last-minute errands to run, so he agreed to meet us at the airport.*

The chauffeur opens the door, and Tevah gets in. I take one last look at the house before I go on my next adventure of life. I'm going to miss this place. Mom stands on the porch with her hand on her hip while Dad carries our bags to the trunk.

It took thirty minutes to calm Mom down from crying earlier.

Tevah says, "Mom didn't cry when I left. Spoiled ass."

The girl in the red buggy stayed for several hours last night after I invited her inside. She attempted to start the car, but this time, I caught her before she could drive away. Her mother told her never to come to Mount Forty, but as soon as she found our address, she took her mom's car even before she got her license, but she was too scared to knock. Her name is Autumn Gray Dunmore, the daughter of my father. The same little girl being held by the lady with the pink hair in my drawing, except she's seventeen now. Dad cut her mother off because he didn't want my mom to find out but has always sent money—that was their arrangement. The man Autumn called father broke things off with her mother and confessed he wasn't her biological father, which urged her to search for my dad.

Tevah and I exchanged phone numbers with her, and Mom and Dad asked her to visit again for dinner.

I feel heat on the side of my neck. I look to the right. There's Todd standing on his mother's porch four houses down. The sky is a gloomy blue, and I can see him watching my every move. The last time I saw him, Tevah and I were destroying his apartment. The way he stands there watching with no expression is creepy.

Dad turns to see what I'm looking at and frowns. "I'm going to blow his fucking head off if he keeps looking over here."

"Why is Todd staring at us? I got a few words for him!" says Tevah, and she steps one leg out of the limo. I place my palm on her wrist.

"Tevah, let's go. Dad, leave it alone. Do not worry about Todd." Tevah looks up at me and takes a nice, long *woo-sah* breath. She scoots back in the limousine.

"Maybe it's time to choose my battles a little better," she says. "That's a great idea, sister."

✳ ✳ ✳

Tevah and I are sitting in a sea of luxury. The leather recliner chairs are tan with back massagers built-in. The flight attendant is a tall, butterscotch lady with the cutest twist-out curls I've ever seen. I wish I could get my curls that defined. Her perfectly round, honeydew cleavage is on the verge of bursting out of her white uniform, and her face is ready for glamour shots. I wonder if Cash hand picked her out of a catalog. So far, they have great service.

We haven't taken off yet, and the flight attendant supplied me with a warm blanket and hot chocolate before I knew I wanted it. I know this isn't the ideal way to handle this kind of situation, and I don't expect everyone to understand, but I have to. I know I will break, and when it does hit me, it will hit me hard. But I can no longer stay in that house. I was surrounded by so much turmoil and distrust, and I am officially tired. I don't want to face this now. I don't want to face this tomorrow or the day after. And I don't think I will ever be ready when reality stares me in the face. But for now, I'm moving forward.

Cash steps on the plane, looking even better than yesterday. He has on a black dress shirt with a few buttons undone to show off his tattoos, and his shiny, white teeth almost blind me with his charming smile. My stomach drops. A guy walks in after Cash. He has on black sweatpants, a black sweat jacket, and he's playing with a toothpick with his tongue. It's Bryson.

Why do I put myself in these situations? Of course he would be on this plane. He told me at the boxing gym he was only in town for a few days, but I thought he was going back to Texas.

"Hey, are you being taken care of?" Cash says, being so attentive and authoritative at the same time.

"Yeah, I can stay on this plane forever," Tevah says as the seat massager vibrates her words. She lifts her glass flute. "I'll take some champagne, ma'am!" Cash snickers, showing off his perfect smile.

"Yes, Cash. We're good. Thank you for inviting us," I say.

"Nice to see y'all beautiful ladies," says Bryson. He reaches over to shake Tevah's free hand. Next, he squeezes my hand, searching in my eyes.

"Hang in there," he sympathetically says.

Hang in there? That's exactly what I need to hear right now. I have yet to lose one tear, and I haven't broken down after finding out what happened to me, and as much as I want to let the river break my levy of pain, I inhale, suck it in, and swallow. I carry my heart in two pockets over what my brother did to me, but I know when that time comes, it will hit when I least expect it. Bryson kisses my hand.

"I will," I whisper. His eyes are a galaxy green with the shades of brown around the rim. It's like he's looking through me. I don't know what this is between us, but it scares me.

Bryson's gentle kiss to my hand sends electricity straight down between my thighs. *How'd he do that? This guy is dangerous. My body recognizes his touch. Scary.*

Cash is talking, but I can't focus on what he's saying.

Bryson is holding a crafty yellow-and-brown daisy box, which looks homemade. It's beautiful. He doesn't look like the kind of guy who's into arts and crafts. He's got a good grip on it too. I know this is crazy to think right now, but what if my music box is in there? *What the hell am I talking about? Whatever fling we had was over before it started.*

Bryson walks about eight feet and looks at the seat to the right. He chooses the aisle seat, which is diagonal to me.

Cash pulls out a long, rectangular pack of Red Vines licorice from his back pocket. "I'm sorry I'm late, but I wanted to pick you up some myself." He passes it to me.

My eyes brighten. "That's sweet of you, Cash. Thank you." He smiles and walks to the seat across from Bryson.

I've never experienced a plane ride this awkward before. We've been in the air twenty minutes, and Bryson hasn't said anything.

Tevah falls asleep ten minutes into the flight, probably because we spent the night talking about our new sister and how we could invite her over once we settled into our apartment. I can only see the back of Cash's head sitting up there. His thick headphones are on, and he's bobbing his head, probably to new music he created. *Am I wrong for feeling the way I do? Is there a guy code of conduct or something?* Bryson looks back at me, and his stare is intense, speaking volumes without saying anything at all. *What does he want to say?* Whatever the case is, there's something about him that draws me in. I don't know why, but I want to jump out of this seat and throw myself into his arms. *Is it because he's the reason for the warm sensation in my chest? Is it because being in his arms will protect me?* Whatever it is, I need it... I crave it... I desire it. As much as I try to give myself a pep talk about how it's time to focus on me and my career right now, it doesn't change the fact that I want Bryson as much as I wanted that chocolate milkshake yesterday. And there's no way I can sprinkle salt on this infatuation to make it go away. I can taste him at the tip of my tongue. And there's nothing I can do about it. But we can never be together now. I know this, and I'm sure Bryson knows too.

Cash walks to the front, and he's talking to the flight attendant. Bryson gets up and treads my way.

Bryson puts a square piece of folded magazine

paper on my food tray.

I throw him a suspicious look, and he nods, telling me to read it. He walks back to his seat and uses the remote control to flip on the flat-screen television on the cabinet wall, and a football game comes on. I unravel the folded magazine paper. In the white space below the clothing ad are words written in black ink.

It reads:

We have unfinished business, Rose.

Check out Part Two of the Hidden Trilogy!

Hidden In Front of Me

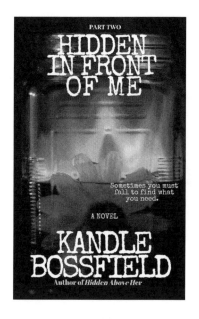

ABOUT THE AUTHOR

KANDLE BOSSFIELD is an American Author that grew up in Sacramento, California. She has two children and has a passion for creativity, writing, and young entrepreneurship. You can follow her @kandlebossfield on Facebook and Instagram. Don't forget to leave an honest book review!

Made in the USA
Las Vegas, NV
10 January 2021